The Age of Longing

The Age of Longing

A NOVEL

Richard B. Wright

A Phyllis Bruce Book
HarperCollins*PublishersLtd*

First edition

Canadian Cataloguing in Publication Data

Wright, Richard B., 1937-
The age of longing : a novel

ISBN 0-00-224408-X (bound)
ISBN 0-00-648067-5 (pbk.)

I. Title.

PS8595.R6A65 1995   C813'.54   C94-932377-2
PR9199.3.W75A65 1995

95 96 97 98 99 ❖ EB 10 9 8 7 6 5 4 3 2 1

Printed and bound in the United States

For my sons
Christopher and Andrew

Against the sustained tick of a watch, fiction takes the measure of a life, a season, a look exchanged, the turning point, desire as brief as a dream, the grief and terror that after childhood we cease to express. The lie, the look, the grief are without permanence. The watch continues to tick where the story stops.

— *What Is Style?*
Mavis Gallant

The Age of Longing

WHEN I WAS THREE or four years old, I used to look for the Stanley Cup in my mother's china cabinet. This search arose from perhaps my earliest memory: my father is holding me under one arm while I grip the basin of a drinking fountain in Little Lake Park. With his free hand, my father presses the lever, and looking down I am both astonished and delighted by the cold water gushing from the white mica ball. Around me are the cries and laughter of the bathers and my mother's voice, insistent and hectoring, the voice of the schoolteacher who is used to issuing instruction or admonition.

"Be careful, Ross! Don't let his mouth touch that!"

For my mother, polio germs lurked everywhere, but especially in places touched by the lips of strangers. Drinking thirstily, I hear too the voices of children nearby.

"That's Buddy Wheeler. He played for Montreal and he won the Stanley Cup."

They are talking about the man who is holding me, my father. And where then was this cup he had won? Why was it not with the other cups in the kitchen cupboard or the china cabinet? Of course, those children got it slightly wrong as most of us do when we hear stories. My father did play four games in the National Hockey League with Montreal. But it was the year *after* they won the Stanley Cup. And I am referring to a Montreal team that is now only a glimmering memory for a few old people. They were called the Maroons.

This summer I returned to my mother's house to begin the sober task of tidying up after death. Even the frugal gather around them a remarkable array of possessions over a lifetime, and after sixty years a house is bound to be filled with things. Before others can move in and begin a life here, there must be a general clearing out. So much has to be retrieved from drawers and closets and then discarded. The lamps and beds, the chairs and tables can be sold to the second-hand furniture people, but no one wants an old woman's shoes or camisoles. They must be cast away, along with the blouses and cardigans, the cough syrup and hand cream, the scarves and winter coats, the jars of pickles in the cellar, the box of baking soda in the refrigerator; it all must go into garbage bags which I carry out to the street each Thursday. It is an arduous and depressing business for a middle-aged man who is trying to recover his health.

Improbable as it may sound, my mother and I both had heart attacks in the same week; as a matter of fact, they occurred within a day of each other, and Mother's, of course, was fatal. That was to be expected perhaps, for she was in her eighty-third year. The circumstances surrounding her death were rather gruesome; apparently she collapsed while preparing her breakfast and lay undetected on the kitchen floor for three days. It was June and unusually warm for early summer. Normally a neighbour looked in on her every day, but during that particular week she was out of town. It was just one of those bits of bad luck where a vicious irony seems to prevail over a sense of decency and order that against all evidence many still imagine to exist. By that I mean that it was not a fitting end to Mother's life. One could justifiably say, I suppose, that decomposing on a kitchen floor in the heat of early summer is scarcely an appropriate conclusion to anyone's life. But for Mother it was especially savage in its irony, for above all other virtues, her Presbyterian soul yearned most after order and tidiness. She was the sort of person who, after her evening bowl of bran flakes, washed and dried the spoon and dish before retiring. Her cheque-book on the top shelf of the secretary in the front hallway was accurate to the day she died. Her corpse was eventually discovered by a fellow from the gas company who had come in to clean the furnace.

I knew nothing of this for several days because I was confined to intensive care in the Toronto Hospital. My "coronary incident," as Dr. Khan insists on calling it, happened about nine in the morning, just before our sales conference for the fall list. I was alone in the washroom drying my hands, probably rehearsing (I can't remember) what I was going to say to the sales staff about my three books. I have done this sort of thing hundreds of times in my thirty years in publishing, though never without that surge of anxiety that always accompanies performance. So,

I was drying my hands on the stiff white cloth of the roller towel when I felt suddenly burdened by a terrible fatigue. It seemed as though a great weight were pressing against me from within and my skin felt greasy. When I looked in the mirror, I was appalled at my pale sweating face. Stepping carefully into one of the cubicles, I sat on a toilet seat cover, where I was found by a colleague and rushed to the hospital. I am enormously grateful for not being able to recall the melodrama of that trip in the ambulance with its siren and revolving light.

My illness then prevented me from going to the funeral which was sparsely attended. No surprise there. Mother made few friends in her life, and most of them had preceded her to the grave. She was one (I am another) who seemed to need few people around. Her last years in particular were almost completely solitary and she was not unhappy. I received a letter from the minister who buried her. A few months earlier Mother had told me that Knox Church now had a new man. He was, she said, "a little too evangelical to suit me." He would be the ninth man in the pulpit since she set foot in Knox Presbyterian Church as a child during the First World War.

295 Park Street
Huron Falls, Ontario
L4R 1R9

June 20, 1994

Mr. Howard Wheeler
Room 427
The Toronto Hospital
200 Elizabeth Street
Toronto, Ontario
M5G 2C4

Dear Mr. Wheeler:

It is with great sadness that I write to tell you of
your mother's passing. A Mrs. Collins gave me
your home and business numbers, and when I
could not reach you at your residence, I phoned
your place of business and spoke to a Ms. Macklin. She informed me of your sudden and unfortu-
nate illness, and I send you my very best wishes for
a speedy recovery, and the hope that God will bless
you at this trying time in your life. Your mother's
funeral was Monday. It was a beautiful summer
day here in Georgian Bay. Although the service
was not greatly attended, it was, I venture to suggest, moving. I chose 1 Corinthians, Chapter 15,
where Paul speaks of God's gift of everlasting life.

For since by man came death, by man came also the resurrection of the dead. For as in Adam all die, even so in Christ shall all be made alive.

Between you and I, Mr. Wheeler, I did not have the opportunity to know your mother very well. I have only been serving now at Huron Falls for three months. But I did greet your mother each Sunday after worship and fully intended to get around to seeing her on my home visits. Unfortunately time did not permit this. I had the impression, however, that your mother was a very independent person who provided leadership and learning to generations of schoolchildren in Huron Falls.

I am sure that she was a kind and caring person, and I imagine that hundreds of young people now grown to adulthood remember her with great affection.

I am sorry to learn of your double misfortune and I certainly hope that you are feeling better soon. When you have recovered and find yourself in Huron Falls, I hope you will drop by and say hello. Karen and I would be delighted to meet you.

Yours faithfully,

Barry Lawson, B.A., D.M.

I have inherited, no doubt from my mother, a critical disposition; over the years it has been useful in my vocation as book editor, though it has caused some distress in my life and certainly in the lives of those who have had to share time and space with me. Still, *between you and I?* You would think that a man of the cloth with a university education would have a better grasp of fundamental grammar. Mr. Lawson is also wrong about Mother. I am referring to that part of his letter in which he imagines her to have been a kind and caring person. Those are not exactly the words that come to mind when I attempt to describe her. Responsible and diligent are perhaps closer to the mark. Sober and critical and unsparing might do just as well. Certainly she did not inspire affection in her pupils, and I grew up under the shadow of their resentment over her forbidding manner in the classroom. I had few friends. As a child, Halloween was a night of watchful and humiliating anxiety. What would some of my schoolmates do to our property? Soap the windows? Scatter our garbage cans? Paint an obscenity on the garage door? Someone once left a human turd on a piece of newspaper on our veranda.

Only the other day I was thinking of the perpetrator of that vile act. It was during one of my walks along the streets of this town where I spent the first eighteen years of my life. Dr. Khan insists that I walk a brisk two miles a day as part of my recovery program. I was thinking during my walk that the person who deposited the excrement on our doorstep fifty or so years ago may very likely still be around. He would be my own age or slightly older, perhaps even the son or younger brother of the man who stopped me outside the legion. He was gruff and elderly, dressed in tan pants, work shirt and a Blue Jays cap. One of those quarrelsome old men whose age now protects him from the blows that he doubtless provokes and deserves each day in the beer hall. We stood talking under the sunlight of an August afternoon.

"You're Buddy Wheeler's boy, aren't you?" he asked, his fierce blue eyes fixing me in a glare.

When you are in your late fifties, it is something to be still called a boy. Yet that remains a custom among those who grow old here. People like myself who leave are forever denied an adult identity. Whatever happened to us after we left town is never taken into account; unless we have made a name for ourselves in some flamboyant manner, we are permanently locked into the town's collective memory as offspring. To a few hardy souls around Huron Falls, I will always be no more and no less than Buddy Wheeler's boy. The old fellow wanted to take me into the legion for a glass of beer, but I had groceries to buy. Still, like Coleridge's Mariner, the old man held me with his glittering eye.

"Someone told me you were back in town and living in your mother's house. She passed away, eh! She must have been up there?"

"Eighty-two," I said.

"I knew your dad," he said. "A helluva hockey player. He could have gone some place. We all thought he would when he went up to Montreal. But he liked a good time too. We all knew that."

Under the bill of the Blue Jays cap, this chronicler of village lore offered me a sly grin before the habitual glare returned.

"I bought a car from your father in nineteen thirty-nine. Just before the war. At old George Fowler's garage over on Bay Street. Fowler Motors. Your father worked there as a salesman. I don't know if you remember him working there. It was a grey Plymouth coupe. A 1935 Plymouth. That son of a bitch was a good little car. She ran right through the war, and you know what?"

"What?"

"I sold her for more than I paid for her in nineteen forty-seven or forty-eight. Sold her to a farmer out in Lafontaine. A helluva little car. I watched your father play hockey hundreds of times up at the old rink. Christ, could he skate! There wasn't anybody around here who could touch him, I can tell you that."

Yes, Buddy Wheeler could skate. He could drink Old Stock Ale and Old Dominion rye too and play softball and cribbage and sell a 1935 Plymouth coupe now and then. He was also what used to be called a natty dresser, favouring checked sports jackets and two-toned shoes. He sang while shaving in a fine tenor voice.

> *Oh the buzzing of the bees*
> *In the cigarette trees*
> *Round the soda-water fountain.*

Like many men nowadays, I live and work among women.

But my father inhabited a male world of cold arenas and beer parlours, of men with old-fashioned names like Chester and Ernie and Wilf. In his world, women stayed in the kitchen or the bedroom, summoned only when needed. Most women, that is; my mother had a job and each morning left her sleeping husband and walked to Dufferin Street Public School.

People continually surprise you even in death. Mother, for example, was one of the least sentimental persons I have ever known. Not for her the calendar from the local dairy with its picture of kittens or cocker spaniel puppies. She would scissor away such images and hang on the kitchen wall only the sheets of large black numbers that recorded the days of the month and the phases of the moon. Not for her the *Warsaw* Concerto which for a time while I was growing up seemed to be blaring from the radio every day. Her favourite composers were Beethoven and Brahms, with Arturo Toscanini conducting the NBC Symphony Orchestra. The packages of heavy black discs came through the mail from the music department of the T. Eaton Company in Toronto.

Mother went through the rituals of Christmas, but she took little joy from the season. She seemed altogether happier to get back to the uncluttered days of January with their promise of new beginnings and fresh resolutions. Improvement in one's character was always very much on her mind. That makes it particularly difficult to understand why she married my father, unless, as I suspect, she felt she could change his ways. What follies in this life can be charged to such ambitions! All her days my mother was uneasy with physical contact; her one concession in greeting or parting was to offer a cool dry cheek that smelled faintly of Camay soap. Yet in the large trunk that once belonged to her father and which stood for years in the closet of her bedroom are the most sentimental objects of all — old photographs and a bundle of letters from my father. The rest of the house has not a trace of the man who left it forever in the summer of the year the Second World War ended.

The letters are from the early days of their marriage when my father was away playing professional hockey. There is a picture of him with another fellow; they are next to a model "A" Ford. Men used to enjoy being photographed near these old machines. My father has a foot up on the running board and an arm across the roof of the car, a lithe handsome man with a shock of blond hair across his brow. He is grinning at the camera during the worst year of the Great Depression. He looks neat and tidy in his white shirt and trousers. My father liked good clothes, and even in his declining years when alcohol had ravaged him and he was a gaunt figure staring out the window of the New American Hotel on Roncesvalles Avenue in Toronto, he was careful about his appearance. His white shirt looked freshly laundered and the French cuffs were folded back across his forearms. In the photograph taken twenty-one years earlier, he grins at the camera in another clean shirt. The other fellow is sitting on the running board, wearing a flat tweed cap and smoking a cigarette. They look like a pair of hold-up men. On the back of the picture someone has scribbled September 1933. My father was twenty-one years old.

When this picture was taken, my mother had already finished her first year of teaching. There is a picture of her here too. It is the teaching staff of Dufferin Street Public School, circa 1932. My mother and three other women stand behind a stout elderly man who is seated on a chair with his hands on his knees. I say elderly, though when this photograph was taken he was probably no older than I am now. I remember him, Mr. Ball, the principal, and I also remember the two other women, Miss Hepworth and Miss King, both of whom taught me in the early grades. My mother is only twenty in the photograph, but she seems older. She is a good head taller than the others, a severe-looking young woman with her dark hair cropped short and her back very straight. She appears to be giving notice to the world that she regards life as a serious business.

Let me tell you that this heart attack has frightened me. Most of us, if we are even remotely aware of ourselves as mortal beings, realize that on some Wednesday morning or Sunday afternoon in some year of our personal histories we shall die. But unless we are possessed of a particularly acute (some might say morbid) sensibility, that peculiar day exists in a future that seems to lie beyond our imagining. Until, that is, we are stricken by the cancerous bowel, the cerebral hemorrhage, the "coronary incident." Then we are swiftly reminded of our fragile state; then it is borne home how quickly the pilot light can go out. And so at my age there persists a longing to understand some things.

Here, for example, in my mother's house, amid the remnants of her life, I am perplexed by the mystery of the union of my father and mother. How could two people who were so very different decide to spend a life together?

John Ross Wheeler travelled with a crowd that had an unsavoury reputation. There were dances at Sandy Beach Pavilion with bottles of rye whisky passed around. Afterwards, or so rumour had it, naked young men and women were to be seen running along the beach and laughing as they plunged into the dark waters of Georgian Bay. The young women who swam with the softball players cleaned houses around town or worked at the looms in the woollen mill until they got pregnant and married. The adjective used often to describe them in those days was "fast."

But Grace Stewart lived in a big house on Park Street with her widowed father. She read library novels and listened to the "Bell Telephone Hour" on the radio. She sent away to the T. Eaton Company for phonograph records of serious music. She taught school and took long, solitary walks in Little Lake Park. Each Sunday morning with her father she attended Knox Presbyterian Church. When she was twenty-two, she astonished many people in town, including her father, by buying her own house, the house I am sitting in at this moment.

What on earth then could have inspired Grace Stewart and Buddy Wheeler to imagine that they could share a satisfying life together? But then, could one not ask the same question of many of us?

Mother never spoke of her courtship or of the early

days of her marriage; in fact, my father's name was seldom mentioned to me in this house after he left to play senior hockey in Nova Scotia in September 1945. No notice of their marriage exists in the *Huron Falls Times* and this is probably because they eloped. They were married in a civil ceremony in Toronto on Labour Day weekend in 1934. Nor, for those of you who think the worst of others, was my mother pregnant at the time. I did not arrive until late July the following year.

As an editor who has worked with writers on biographies of notable sporting figures, egomaniacal tycoons, political scoundrels and other worthies in our nation's story, I have often wondered about this process of fashioning truth, admittedly an elusive term, out of past events. How do we know what really happened? There are the facts of course: Grace Stewart and John Ross Wheeler were married at City Hall on Friday, August 31, 1934. According to the *Toronto Daily Star*, it was an overcast day with intermittent periods of rain: a day for opening and closing umbrellas or running from shop to lunch counter with a folded newspaper over your head. But facts alone explain nothing. They are merely there. What surrounds those facts is another matter altogether and one that is far more intriguing. Perhaps we could call it surmise and allow it a place in any accounting of events.

My parents' marriage certificate, for instance, bears the signatures of a justice of the peace, J. O. Symington, and a Mrs. I. Crosley as witness. Mrs. I. Crosley? Irma? Ida? Irene? Iris? And why did a married woman have a job at

City Hall in 1934? It would have been unusual unless, as I suspect, Mrs. Crosley was a widow, who got her job through her late husband's affiliation with the Orange Order.

What went through Mrs. Crosley's mind, I wonder, as she watched the tall, plain girl and her young man with his blond cowlick and boyish grin utter the words of life-long commitment to each other? Mrs. Crosley must certainly have noticed that the young woman appeared to be in charge of things; it was she who had arranged matters by letter and paid the clerk. The young man seemed content enough to be carried along by events; an amiable spectator but too good-looking for Miss Stewart who was probably pregnant. In Mrs. Crosley's view, there would doubtless be trouble down the road. But when wasn't there trouble? Wasn't trouble what you should expect in this life? Well, perhaps. We shall never know what Mrs. Crosley thought, if anything at all, about the little ceremony that took place on an overcast Friday afternoon in the late summer of 1934.

THERE ARE NOW THREE women in my life and each of them in her own way is looking after me. Mrs. Chernyk is a Hungarian lady in a canary-coloured pantsuit who is trying to sell this house for me. I got her name from the phone book, and she came around one morning a few weeks ago, and with swift, sure strokes hammered a For Sale sign into the front lawn. Mrs. Chernyk dislikes the unions and the socialists. She has opinions. She believes, for instance, that Canadians are spoiled and self-indulgent.

"You people do not know what difficulties are. You should have been in my country when the Russians came with their tanks."

How can I disagree with her? I have never faced a tank in my life.

From time to time, usually in the evenings, Mrs. Chernyk will bring a young couple around to see the house. During these visits, I try to make myself as inconspicuous as possible, hastily clearing away my supper dishes. Standing in the hallway, I listen to the footsteps overhead and to Mrs.

Chernyk's voice as she tries to disarm the criticisms of prospective buyers: "Yes, there is only one bathroom, but look at the size of it! And a shower and toilet in the basement is no problem. I know a man who does such things at a very reasonable cost."

So far, however, Mrs. Chernyk has been unsuccessful. For these young couples, the house is too old and too big; there are stairs to climb and hardwood floors to polish and only one bathroom. It came as news to me that people nowadays seem unable to survive with only one bathroom. Yet Mrs. Chernyk remains hopeful; I suppose she must to prevail in her trade.

"Do not concern yourself, Mr. Wheeler," she will say each time we stand on the veranda and watch another young couple drive away. "I know my business, and I will find a buyer for your mother's house."

The second woman in my life these days is my boss Linda Macklin who phoned this morning. Linda has been editorial director at Caedmon House now for six months. She was brought in after several highly successful years with another firm to succeed my former boss, Del Shannon, who perished from AIDS, poor man. Linda does not have a high opinion of me as an editor despite my thirty years in the business, and that is why I am surprised that she has asked me to read the Pettinger manuscript. I think Linda sees me as something of a nonentity, and with my old-fashioned specs and striped shirts with their detachable collars and the bow ties, a fussy and rather unprepossessing person. Every publishing house used to have at least one Howard Wheeler toiling away in its editorial offices. Del Shannon used to say that gents like me were part of a vanishing breed. It always made me feel a bit antiquated when he said that. Del liked me; he recognized that I was a competent if unspectacular editor, and over the years I heard how he often went to bat for me against enemies. People like me have now been replaced by younger, more aggressive types, usually female, which by the way I do not resent. I like women, though for months Linda was under the impression that I was an old gay caballero. It came as quite a shock when I told her during a luncheon conversation that I was resolutely heterosexual and indeed had been married and have a son and daughter.

For the past twenty years, however, I have lived as a bachelor fulfilling one of my mother's many prophecies regarding my fate.

"I doubt you will ever marry, Howard," she once said. "You're too much like me. You enjoy being by yourself and you are too easily set in your ways."

Who knows where such pronouncements can lead to in the young? Not long afterwards, I met and married the airline stewardess and did not live happily ever after.

I was getting ready to go out to escape the noise of the vacuum cleaner upstairs when Linda phoned. Standing in the hallway by my mother's little secretary, I looked out at the front walk and street through the panes of coloured glass that form a border around the oval window of the front door. As a child I had stood there on many winter afternoons gazing out at the snow and the trees through the ruby- or amber-coloured light. It was a favourite pastime. Linda sounded cheerfully brusque, a style that has been interpreted by writers and media people as direct and honest and helpful. In a recent Sunday newspaper profile, she was described as "a no-nonsense person who does not suffer fools gladly." Perhaps that is why she often seems impatient with me, though since my illness this impatience has assumed a mildly condescending form. I am a poor old thing on the way out and must be accorded at least a fundamental civility.

"Howard?" she asked. "How are you? Are you looking after yourself?"

"I am on the mend, Linda, I think."

"Great! Howard, listen! You are not going to believe this, but we've just received Charles Pettinger's novel."

"Pettinger? Good heavens!"

"Yes, exactly. I thought he was dead or had given up writing."

"Well, it must be twenty years since *Unholy Wars*."

"Almost to the day. Listen, Howard! Can you read this thing for us?"

"Well, of course, I'll be glad to." A Pettinger manuscript had always been a job for Del Shannon and the executive board. I would read it for interest after all the decisions had been made.

"It's a monster, Howard," said Linda. "Two boxes. There must be three hundred thousand words."

"A long time a-borning," I said. "The man obviously has his story to tell."

"Well, maybe," she said, "but I don't see how we could possibly do it alone. We'd almost certainly need help from New York with the costing."

She sounded mildly exasperated, and I could see her at the keyboard of her VDT with the phone tucked into her shoulder as she accessed the names of those in the company who have birthdays this week. Linda then sends everyone a little "personal note" by E-mail.

"You will be a dear and read this thing, Howard? Say no if you're not up to it, but we really would value your opinion."

That was a bit thick, but I was still excited by the prospect. Charles Pettinger has been a literary hero of mine for the past twenty-three years.

"Of course," I said. "I'd be delighted."

"Wonderful," said Linda. "I'll have it sent to you by courier within the hour. Do you have Federal Express or UPS up there?"

"I think so, yes. I have seen their trucks."

"Good! Can you get back to us, say in two weeks?"

"I don't see why not."

"Great. Your cheque's here too. I'll send that along with the manuscript."

"Excellent."

I will say this for Linda: she has made certain throughout my ordeal that I have not had to worry about money.

"I have to run, Howard. Another meeting. You know what it's like around here. You're an angel. Take care of yourself."

"Yes. You too, Linda. Goodbye."

I hung up the phone feeling, as I have said, unusually

excited. At Caedmon House we had been waiting for Charles Pettinger's manuscript for two decades. Over that time Del Shannon must have written at least two hundred letters of support and encouragement. The reclusive author's replies were usually one or two lines: "Thanks for your letter, Del. The book is coming along."

Del would show me these with a smile that grew increasingly ironical with each passing year and ended finally in a resigned shrug. Most people who have even a casual acquaintance with Canadian fiction will have heard of Pettinger's first book, *The Rage of the Freeway Driver.* This collection of stories was published in the early 1970s, and immediately established Pettinger as a fresh new voice in literature. The book was extravagantly praised and proved to be one of those rare items in publishing: a critically successful literary work that was also commercially popular. It was translated into many languages, and you will still find it studied in Canadian literature courses throughout the land.

The stories are both funny and serious and they represent a genuine attempt to understand the difficulties of living in a post-Christian world in the last quarter of the century. The characters in these stories are not only baffled by the moral emptiness of materialism but also psychologically cornered by the prospect of finitude. Yet they somehow endure. Pettinger has been labelled with some justification as Canada's Walker Percy, though, of course, Pettinger hasn't been nearly as prolific as the late Southern novelist. Pettinger's second collection of stories, *Unholy*

Wars, published five years later, maintained a similar theme but was less successful. *Unholy Wars* lacked the edge of the first book and there was a noticeable absence of the comic spirit that had so informed *Rage*. A mildly sour note rang throughout, signalling perhaps the author's growing disenchantment with his fellow man. *Unholy Wars* is still a fine book, and it received respectful reviews. It wasn't as if its author had been bludgeoned into silence by criticism. He just seemed to be taking his time with his third book, living on his farm in eastern Ontario with his schoolteacher wife.

For a while in the seventies he gave occasional readings and appeared now and then at writers' conferences and workshops. But gradually he withdrew from any public appearance. From time to time his name would crop up in literary journals, his first book a reference point for some critic's examination of a new writer's stories. Over time, however, his name faded from sight and Charles Pettinger has now become a virtually forgotten figure in Canadian literature; there are probably many who believe, as Linda Macklin did a week ago, that Pettinger is no longer among the living. And now his long silence has been vindicated. It was cheering news and I felt invigorated by it. Happy for the man and for myself. I would soon be back at work.

Turning from the telephone I watched the third woman in my life, Louise Ouellette, manoeuvre her way down the staircase lugging my mother's old Electrolux that looks for all the world like a small bomb. Louise nodded to me as she made her way through to the kitchen. A day or so after returning to Huron Falls, I advertised in the *Times* for someone to clean the house every second Friday. Louise was the first to phone, and when she came around in her ten-year-old LTD with its faulty muffler, I hired her almost at once. I liked the sturdy look of her and she told me that she was dependable, a word you seldom hear any more. It belongs to another age and as a word person I was immediately won over by her use of it. She said I could phone people who knew her, but I never bothered.

Louise knew all about my mother's death, and on that first day she looked around the kitchen. She seemed to be tasting the air, imagining perhaps the decay and awfulness that must have been there when the furnace man looked in through the window. No matter. She is a tough, plucky woman, somewhere in her late thirties I would guess. Her hair is still dark, and in her face I can still see the vestiges of the pretty teenager she once was. In high school I would have cast hopeless looks of adoration at someone like Louise; in my day most of the prettiest girls in Huron Falls were French Canadian. Louise has four children, all between twelve and eighteen. A difficult time for her. The eighteen-year-old daughter is proving to be a handful, and Louise's husband has been laid off at the Mitsubishi factory where he used to assemble TVs. Now he sits at home drinking beer and watching the serial dramas. A worried man, he yells at the kids and at Louise.

She tells me all this when we sit on the back stoop during one of her breaks. She pulls up her knees and leans against the clothesline pole and enjoys a smoke. She wears jeans and running shoes and one of her son's old hockey sweaters while we talk about how difficult life can be. While Louise talks, I stare out at the back lawn that again needs cutting and at the remains of my mother's last garden; the carrots and beets and runner beans have been strangled by the weeds. It looks untidy, a lazy man's late summer garden, and the place would probably be more saleable if I had someone dig it all up. I am also fond of Louise because, at some point in our first meeting, she told me that before she was married her name was Fournier. I then asked if her father or an uncle perhaps had played hockey. She told me that her grandfather used to play and her two sons were now into minor hockey and the cost of skates and equipment was terrible, et cetera, et cetera.

I went at once to my mother's bedroom and returned with a picture of the Huron Falls Flyers, the Intermediate A team that went to the provincial semifinals in 1935. My father sits in the front row between the coach, Buck Houle, and the team's owner, George Fowler. Leo Fournier, a big, dark-haired defenceman, stands in the back row. He is Louise's grandfather.

Handing her the picture I was foolishly moved by the symmetry of it all: there we were over fifty years later, direct descendants of two figures in a grainy old photograph. But Louise found nothing remarkable in that. To her it was just another old picture. Which of course was true. She looked at it for a moment before handing it back.

"Yeah, that's him," she said. "Cranky old bugger!"

She then told me that her grandfather is still alive and living out his days in Birchmount Lodge. I intend to visit him and ask about my father.

Today, after Louise washes and waxes the kitchen floor, scrubbing the death out of it, so to speak, we have a beer together on the back porch. Today we talk about money. Louise is always concerned about money as who amongst us isn't? The kids will soon be going back to school and will need new clothes. The LTD is nearly shot and what will they do for a car then? Her husband won't talk about any of this. Louise tells me that she dreams of winning the lottery. It is what she thinks about every night before she goes to sleep. If she wins, she would like to take her husband to Las Vegas for a holiday.

It is very agreeable sitting on the back stoop on this late summer morning and watching Louise. Now and then I steal a sidelong glance at her while she talks. She drinks her beer straight from the bottle, tilting back her head. I look at her fine brown throat. Beneath the hockey sweater she wears a black brassiere and I am still able to be stirred by such a sight, though in the arms of a woman like Louise Ouellette I would fear for my heart.

It seems to me that women nowadays are stronger than they used to be. Most of them at the office spend their lunch hours at the YWCA jogging on the cork track. They leave with their gym bags and towels looking as alert and purposeful as young disciples. I have watched Linda Macklin straining against doorjambs and windowsills while she talks. Some kind of isometric thing, I suppose. I am sure that any of these women could wrestle me to the floor in an instant.

AFTER LOUISE OUELLETTE LEAVES, the house smells of floor wax and furniture polish. I climb the stairs to sit in the rocking chair in my mother's bedroom at the front of the house. Her bedroom faces west onto Queen Street, and so the sun is now at the back of the house and the heat of the day has not yet risen to the second floor. Here it is still cool under the leafy trees and shadowy sunlight. As a child, I seldom came into this room. It wasn't exactly forbidden, but it seemed somehow inviolate. Mother's room! My view of the neighbourhood was mostly from my bedroom window at the rear of the house overlooking the backyards and the garages in the laneway that separates the properties along Queen and Maple streets. Whenever I looked out on Queen Street, it was from the parlour or through the coloured glass of the front door window. This view from my mother's bedroom then offers another angle on the familiar. It's a bit like sitting in the back seat of your car; the surroundings are the same, but they look different.

Across the street a young man is spraying a lawn. He wears rubber boots and gloves and walks back and forth with his hose. When he finishes, he sticks little signs into the grass warning of possible harm from the chemicals. His work will doubtless keep the dandelions away next spring. Watching him coil his hose onto the back of the truck, I think of my mother who knelt on the lawn each May, and with the end of a teaspoon levered out the dandelion roots. Such tedious tasks did not seem to confound her generation.

I have stripped her bed, and looking across the room to where she lay alone each night since September 1945, I now regret it. A bare mattress is an unseemly sight, a naked rebuke to eighty years of life. I may very likely have been conceived on that bed.

I have tried to imagine how my parents met. A chance remark by my father one night in the Nanking Tavern in Toronto provided a clue, but even my Aunt Mildred, my father's youngest sister and the one closest to him, couldn't remember when I asked her some years ago before she died. All she said was, "I really can't remember, Howard. One weekend near the end of summer they just turned up married. It sure took us all by surprise."

I like to imagine that my parents met on the evening mother decided to buy this house. A warm evening in early July, and she went out after supper, leaving her father reading the paper in one of the wicker chairs on the veranda of the big house on Park Street. She is glad to get away, for the two of them have not been getting along for some time. The old man is becoming increasingly cranky, his ill temper aggravated by a persistent ache in his lower spine.

Most nights he sleeps only fitfully. Unknown to him or his daughter, it is cancer and it will kill him within three years.

On this July evening then, Grace Stewart walks along Park Street. Her neighbours watch her pass from their lawns and verandas. They regard her as an unusual young woman who perhaps keeps too much to herself. Most think she is destined for spinsterhood. And isn't it a good thing she has the teaching! She'll be like Miss King or Miss Hepworth, plain pennies all!

"There goes Grace for her walk" is how one elderly lady across the street probably put it as she watched my mother leave the house. But Grace Stewart is not just going for a walk; instead she is doing something rather extraordinary for a single woman of twenty-two in the year 1934.

For the past several weeks she has been looking at houses to buy, and in fact has come upon the very one she wants. She has had her eye on it for some time now, and it quickens her heart just to think of owning it. How she will tell her father about all this is something she prefers not to think about at the moment. She is determined, however, to be settled in this house by the start of the school year. How will she pay for it? She has been left a legacy of two thousand dollars by Aunt Julia, her father's sister. The price of houses has plunged over the past three years, and it is a shrewd time to buy if you can handle a mortgage. With all this in mind, she is meeting Fred Robinson of Barnes and Robinson at six-thirty.

While she walks across town to Queen Street, Buddy Wheeler, according to the local paper and its sports editor,

Chip McNeil, "lined a sharp single to right field scoring Russ Wilson in the third inning." The *Huron Falls Times* records that on this Thursday evening, Huron Falls met Hillfield and won 7-4. Buddy Wheeler played first base and batted clean-up. He went three for five, driving in four runs. So, while Buddy is playing softball, Grace is thinking of how agreeable it will be to live in this house. The neighbourhood is not as grand as Park Street, but it is solid and respectable. Best of all, she will now be only a ten-minute walk from school. The twenty-year-old maples and oaks along the street have already grown into handsome shade trees.

The house itself was built in 1909 of red brick with a wrap-around veranda covered now with vines of Dutchman's-pipe. A leafy green retreat on summer afternoons. There are three bedrooms, a bathroom, a large kitchen, dining room and parlour with plenty of cupboard and closet space and a cool dry basement. The backyard is suitable for a vegetable garden and there is a garage belonging to the property in the laneway behind the house. The place has had only two owners, a merchant who had the house built and lived in it with his family for over twenty years until he was ruined by the Depression. And its present owner, a doctor from Toronto who has returned to the city. The story has it that his wife disliked small-town life; they stayed only a short while and the house has been empty now for almost a year.

A house unlived-in soon goes downhill, and standing in the basement by the coal furnace with Fred Robinson, Grace Stewart knows this. The house will need new paint and wallpaper. The doctor's wife was a sloven; you can see that by the grease stains on the wall near the kitchen stove. The floors are yellowing with old wax and the board fence behind the house will need repair. Meanwhile she and Fred Robinson are apart by two hundred dollars. She can sense, however, that the real estate agent is beginning to bend. After all, except for the range and icebox, the furniture is gone and that makes a house more difficult to sell. The fact of the matter is that no one appears to want the place except her. Does that not give her the advantage? She has made him a fair offer. The two hundred dollars can go towards paint and wallpaper and legal fees and goodness knows what else. Beneath Robinson's affable salesman's banter, she can detect an impatient eagerness to be rid of both her and the house. She resents his jokey patronizing manner but she is prepared to let that pass and not unsettle matters with a sharp remark. The main thing is to get the house at her price.

Fred Robinson, known around town as Rusty Robinson because of his sandy-coloured hair and light freckled skin, has been selling houses in Huron Falls for over thirty years with his partner Billy Barnes. During the Second World War, Robinson will be elected mayor of the town for two terms. But now, in the basement of this house on a warm summer evening in 1934, he is both puzzled and irritated by the business before him. It is almost an occupation in itself to keep smiling. He feels downright peculiar standing here trying to sell a house to a girl barely out of school. Why his own daughter graduated from high school with

Grace Stewart and she is still at home! And why does Grace Stewart want this place anyway when she has a perfectly good home to live in over on Park Street? If she wanted to rent the house, he might be able to see that, though she'd have the devil's own time trying to get decent people into it. And if you don't, the place soon goes to blazes. But she told him she doesn't want to rent it; she wants to live in it. Did you ever hear of such foolishness in your life? A young woman by herself in a big house like this? That afternoon it had even passed through Rusty Robinson's mind to give old Jim Stewart a call at the foundry, but he thought better of it. Stewart was such an irritable old cuss that he was likely to hang up in your ear.

The daughter is like her father too. The truth of the matter is that Rusty Robinson can usually abide most folks, but he can't bring himself to like this tall solemn young woman. She has little conversation and no sense of humour. It's a genuine chore to deal with her, he thinks as he watches Grace inspect the fruit cellar, a little cupboard at the far end of the basement. She is looking at some old pickling jars that have doubtless been there for years. Rusty Robinson is also thinking about Friday afternoon when he will board the *Huron Queen* and travel to Honey Harbour for a week-end with his family at the cottage. It will be nice to get away from shirts that cling to your back and empty afternoons listening to the office fan and the clacking of his secretary's typewriter. Business is almost dead this time of year, and getting rid of this place would be a good way to end his week. Yet it rankles him that Grace Stewart, barely out of school, will not budge on her offer. She won't even split the difference of one hundred dollars. Most reasonable people would do that, but not this gawky girl with her frown. It is vexing to deal with such a person though the real estate man knows how to conceal displeasure.

A few minutes later, standing in the parlour where Grace intends one day to put her mother's piano, Rusty Robinson accepts her price and, after securing the front door with a set of tagged keys, offers Grace Stewart a ride home. To his relief, she declines, saying that she would prefer to walk. Touching the brim of his Panama hat, Robinson bids her good evening and, climbing into his Graham-Paige sedan, drives away feeling vaguely unsettled, as we all do when we imagine that we have been outwitted by someone we dislike.

As for Grace, she is quietly exultant. She stuck to her guns and got the house at her price. Not only that, but this purchase also marks a new beginning for her. And are we ever as happy as when we are on the threshold of hope? Are we ever again as amazed and delighted as when we detect the possibility of a sea change in our lives? What if the diet or the plan to read all of Shakespeare lies in tatters six weeks down the road? The night before such enterprises is joy undiminished. During her lifetime my mother embarked on countless voyages of self-improvement: piano and painting lessons, Great Books courses, horticultural projects, vocabulary exercises. She was always happiest during the planning stages of such schemes. And so I imagine her to be on the evening she bought this house as she walked in her purposeful striding manner along Queen Street, turning west on Hannah towards King.

This route takes her close to the fairgrounds and the ball diamond where she hears the crowd in the wooden bleachers. Normally she would not be seen within a hundred paces of a ball game. Why would she? Grace Stewart has no interest whatsoever in sports. Why then, instead of turning right on King Street and heading home, does she cross the street and make her way to the ball diamond? Perhaps it has something to do with all this exultation within her. She may not appear so to others, but she is too pleasantly excited to go directly home and sit with her father who is listening to the radio. And concentrating on a book is out of the question. Tonight she needs diversion in whatever guise. And so she approaches the wooden seats, passing through the knots of people gathered on the sidelines.

She finds an empty seat near the first baseline and sits there, mildly startled by the cheerful clamour in the air. The home team is winning and the crowd is in a good humour. The man beside her, for example, cups his hands to his mouth to intone a kind of chant that Grace finds virtually incomprehensible. He might as well be shouting in a foreign tongue.

"ComeonnowBuddyboy! AttaboyattaboyattaboyBud! GethimBudComeonBud. He'sgotnothin'Bud. AttaboyBud!"

Others around Grace jeer at the pitcher or encourage the batter. But why, she wonders, would anyone get so worked up over a game? It strikes her as mildly outlandish behaviour for adults, and all this coarse, boisterous enthusiasm reminds her of nothing so much as the schoolyard at recess when the boys are shouting and taunting one another at their games. Yet Grace is also fascinated by the fact that someone like Buddy Wheeler can inspire such affection from strangers. Everyone around her is offering up their goodwill to him. Beside her, the man again uses his hands as a kind of megaphone to cry aloud into the darkening air.

"ComeonnowBuddy. ComeonnowBud! He'sgotnothin'Bud. AttaboyBud. Comeonnow!"

Grace watches Buddy Wheeler as he fouls off another pitch. She remembers him from her early days in high school; he seldom did any work and was often late in the morning, entering the classroom by the rear door and sliding into his seat. The teachers mostly ignored him. She can't remember Buddy Wheeler ever answering a question. He left before the end of grade nine. The next year one of his sisters came to the high school. Muriel Wheeler was a couple of years older, a pretty girl who, like her brother, sat at the back of the room, and said not a word all year though in the hallway she seemed talkative enough. By year's end she too had vanished.

There were three Wheeler sisters, Martha, Muriel and Mildred, and they were all popular with the boys. It was said they enjoyed a party. All three would grow into large handsome women, my aunts, who would now and then visit us, particularly during the war when times were good and money a little more plentiful. They would come up from Toronto with their husbands to see old Joe Wheeler who was then in frail health over on Dock Street.

On Sunday afternoons, before returning to the city, they would come by our house. I am sure they regarded it as something of a duty call. In their sleeveless, summer dresses they seemed enormous, greeting me with hugs, their heavy, bare arms enclosing me. I felt overwhelmed by all that flesh. They brought with them Milky Way chocolate bars and balsa-wood model airplane kits that I was too inept to assemble. The boxes lay for years at the bottom of drawers next to my underwear. All three of my aunts married the same type of man: smaller framed with sleek hair smelling of hair oil. They were "sharp dressers," turned out for these occasions in slacks and sports jackets and two-toned shoes. They smoked Buckingham cigarettes or White Owl cigars and sold things for a living: shoes or brushes or magazine subscriptions. One worked a concession at the CNE each year, and another, Aunt Mildred's husband, Uncle Alf, did something at a radio station. They told mildly smutty stories using Scottish or Jewish or Irish dialects. To me, they were exotic and remarkable creatures from another planet.

Mother dreaded these visits. To her, my aunts inhabited a world of rented houses and time payments. They and their husbands exhibited a careless disregard for the future; they were the grasshoppers from the old fable that entreats prudence and thrift in this life. After one of these visits, my mother always forecast their doom.

"When this war is over, and times are tough again, you'll see them on the street without a penny to bless themselves with. You mark my words."

This prophecy was usually delivered to my mother's only confidante during those years, a widow and retired teacher named Mrs. Parker, who came by once or twice a week for tea.

On this summer evening in 1934, however, only Martha is married. She and Muriel, who works in Toronto as a housemaid, are back in Huron Falls for a few days. The youngest, Mildred, still lives at home and works at Woolworth's. They watch their brother hit a grounder to end the Huron Falls inning. Beside Grace, the man's eyes follow Buddy Wheeler as he trots down to first base.

"That'sokayBudboythat'sokaywegot'emnowBud. Three awayBudthreeawaylet'sget'em."

Playing first base, Buddy Wheeler is only a few steps away from the tall, young woman who sits in the front row of the bleachers. He sees her when he turns to wave yet again at his sisters. Her name is Grace Stewart. Her father runs the foundry. Buddy wonders what she is doing here; in her skirt and white blouse she looks somehow out of place. He can remember her from grade nine. She sat at the front of the room and knew all the answers. She was always reading or doing work in her notebooks. A very smart girl. In those days she wore her long dark hair in braids and he saw only the back of her neck. Now she has had her hair cut short, almost like a man's. Yet he likes the look of it.

From time to time he steals a glance at her and in the gathering darkness sees only her pale face and short dark hair and white blouse. How does she look to him? Calm and refined, he supposes. *Educated*. He's heard that she teaches school at Dufferin Street where he went years ago. Buddy watches the first Hillfield batter strike out, and he shouts encouragement to the pitcher and looks again at Grace Stewart. She is so different from the girls who hang around the ball team. *What is she doing here*? Does she like softball? Buddy feels a surge of pride and happiness playing here in the twilight listening to the crowd. But the ball is now a dark bird that can fly past you and die in the grass beyond. And, in fact, the second batter drills a line drive that skips past him and disappears into the outfield. Tagging up, the batter grins at Buddy.

"We're not dead yet, *Buddy boy*!" he says taking his lead.

Buddy ignores him. He knows the fellow. Played hockey against him last winter. Instead Buddy looks over at Grace Stewart and grins.

Everyone is now urging the pitcher to finish it off and he does. The next batter lines the first pitch directly at Buddy who scoops it up with his big mitt, steps on the bag and throws out the runner at second. The small crowd rises to its feet, cheering. Only Grace Stewart, as though unsure of what to do, remains seated. She sits there like some pale emblem while people brush past her, or step down and across seats. Friends and relatives mingle with the players along the sidelines. The Wheeler girls have come down to talk to their brother. You can hear their laughter, and whenever she does hear it in the years that lie ahead, Grace will be moved to wonder how they can possibly find so much in life amusing. It is almost dark now and from across the fairgrounds comes the sound of automobile engines; their yellow headlamps light up the dark grass.

In a sense this is now the moment of my beginning and of my children's and of their children's children. Buddy Wheeler waves to his sisters and walks towards the bleachers and the pale young woman who sits there bemused by the evening and by life's possibilities. Buddy Wheeler is an attractive young man in his baggy, grey uniform with its red piping and the words "Huron Falls" stitched across his chest. He wears his short-billed cap. In a few years I will sit beside him at the kitchen table while he eats his supper in this uniform, his stockinged feet curled around the legs of his chair, the cap hanging on the kitchen doorknob. Resting his foot on her seat, he leans in towards her, his forearm across his knee.

"You're Grace Stewart, aren't you? Didn't I go to school with you? In grade nine?"

Grace nods. She can smell the sweat and the dust on him. Even in this fading light she can see a ring of dirt around his neck, and she would like nothing better than to take a damp warm cloth and erase it. His teeth, she notes, are surprisingly white.

"You were in school with my sister Muriel too," he says. "She said you were always reading books. You always had the answers when the teacher asked."

The perceptions that others have of us can so often promote wonder. Not for a moment had Grace ever imagined that Muriel Wheeler would have given her a thought, let alone talked about her.

"I'm Buddy Wheeler. You want to come out to Sandy Beach for a swim?"

This is a playfully rhetorical question. He knows that this serious quiet girl is not the sort for Sandy Beach. Yet she looks so solemn that he feels like teasing her.

"A bunch of us are going," he says. "It'll be all right. My three sisters will be there. You'll be safe with me, Gracie." He is grinning at her.

Gracie! No one has ever called her Gracie before. Some people, by the force of their temperaments and manner, do not lend themselves to diminutives. Even when she was a child, her parents had never called her Gracie. And she has never been swimming. The thought of appearing half-naked in public is not so much distasteful to her as unimaginable. She has walked among the bathers at Little Lake Park on Sunday afternoons, but she could never see herself as a part of that parade of flesh. To Buddy Wheeler's astonishment, she takes his question seriously, just as she will take all questions in her life seriously.

"Thank you for asking," she says, "but I don't swim."

"You don't swim or you can't swim?" he asks, feigning amusement. "Well I could teach you, Gracie. It's not hard. Everyone should know how to swim."

He is delighted by the grave air surrounding her, and he vaguely senses that she has an inner strength he does not possess. There is about her a resolve that he lacks. He does know that the thought of going out with a schoolteacher is appealing.

"How about going to the show with me on Saturday night, Gracie?" he asks.

Grace is not at all smitten by this good-looking grinning young man who peers so intently at her from out of the near darkness. The Stewarts do not easily give away their hearts; caution and reserve oversee their judgement in all matters. There is no room for caprice in their nature. Yet she is fascinated by the goodwill that Buddy Wheeler gathers around him. He attracts affection and admiration from friend and stranger alike and this quality is foreign to her. To the surprise of both perhaps, she accepts his invitation. She will meet him in front of the Capitol Theatre at 6:45. He laughs.

"The first show, eh, Gracie! I'll have you home before dark. Don't worry."

"I'm not worried," she says.

"That's good," says Buddy, taking off his cap and with the back of his hand wiping his brow. "I'll see you on Saturday in front of the show at a quarter to seven."

She nods and he settles the cap on his head again and walks away to join the others. At one point he stops and looking back waves to her. Grace feels as happy as she has ever felt. She has just bought a house and been asked to the movies by a young man who has suddenly appeared in her life to intrigue her. A summer of planning lies ahead.

ON THE SECOND SATURDAY in July 1934, the Capitol Theatre features Wallace Beery in *Viva Villa* along with a Charlie Chase comedy. Across from the theatre, Buddy sits in a 1919 Ford touring car that belongs to his father. He is watching the rain. After a day of heavy grey heat, the skies have opened to this downpour. The gutters along King Street are running with water and the rain is drumming on the cloth roof of the old automobile. A damp stain is spreading above Buddy's head. The car itself is something of a disgrace: a high, old vehicle on narrow tires, its black paint fading after years of sunlight and winter storms. Buddy's father, Joe Wheeler, uses it as a kind of truck. The back seat has been removed so that all manner of things, tools, old tires, lengths of chain, bags of chicken feed, can be transported. The car has a dank, musty smell and Buddy is mildly ashamed to be seen in it. Still, it's better than getting soaked in the rain.

From time to time Buddy sips from a pint bottle of ginger ale mixed half and half with Old Dominion. After each sip he tucks the bottle under the front seat. Oddly enough, on this humid summer evening, Buddy is thinking of winter. Most people he knows complain about the winter, but he loves those months of cold and snow. He enjoys lying in bed, sore and tired after a hockey game, listening to the wind off the bay hurl the snow against the house. On such nights he sometimes gets up and stands by the window and looks out at the white wildness of it all. In the old "T" he thinks too of the sound and feel of ice underfoot; of winter Saturdays at daybreak when he was the first up to light the kitchen stove and eat his bread and tea and take his skates and stick to the bay behind the coal docks. There as a child he skated for hours in wide sweeping arcs, pushing the lump of coal ahead of him as he stickhandled around imaginary opponents. Later his sisters would join him, playing with makeshift sticks fashioned from tree branches. Martha was tough and strong, and Buddy always thought that if she'd been a man, she would have been a helluva hockey player.

Buddy takes another sip of whisky and ginger ale and wonders why he asked Grace Stewart to the movies. It crosses his mind that he has made a terrible mistake and should now perhaps just forget it and drive away. What will they talk about anyway? He doesn't even have a clear picture in his mind of what she looks like; there is only an impression of this tall serious girl in her white blouse sitting in the bleachers in twilight. Muriel used to say that Grace Stewart was a stuck-up bookworm. Yet when you looked at it from another angle, what did Muriel know? She now cleaned houses for rich people in Toronto while

Grace Stewart taught school. Buddy takes a last nip from the bottle and stows it under the seat.

The rain has now let up and he can hear the thunder rolling northward up the bay towards the islands. A shaft of sunlight strikes the glistening street and the air now feels rinsed and cooler. With the end of the rain, people suddenly appear on the street and a line begins to form in front of the theatre. It is now twenty minutes to seven and Buddy Wheeler wonders whether Grace Stewart will even show up. Maybe she too had second thoughts; after all, she doesn't even know him. Yet Buddy already grasps an elemental truth about the young woman he has asked to the movies on this Saturday night. In that innermost part of him, he knows that she will appear. Without having spoken a hundred words to her, he understands that she is the kind of person who abides by the terms of any agreement, however trivial. This intimation of her unequivocal honesty is both alluring and frightening to him if for no other reason than the fact of its absence thus far in his life.

At that very moment he sees her walking down the street, a tall ungainly young woman wearing a beige raincoat and carrying aloft a large black umbrella. She joins the others in the line and whether from pessimism or forgetfulness continues to hold the umbrella above her. Buddy chews a handful of sen sens and gets out of the car. When he joins her in the line, she seems neither happy nor surprised to see him. They nod shyly at each other and stare ahead while the line inches forward to the ticket booth and the darkened interior of the theatre. Several young men with their girls recognize Buddy and call and wave to him as he and Grace take their seats.

The Charlie Chase comedy involves a domestic misunderstanding with an irate mother-in-law and wife and the hero locked out of his house and subjected to several humiliating ordeals. Most of the audience, including Buddy, find these antics hilarious, and not for the first time or last time will Grace ponder why most people are so easily amused in this life. Others seem to laugh so readily at incidents and anecdotes that she considers merely foolish. Even during the lunch hour at school, Miss King and Miss Hepworth will recall with amusement episodes from radio programs like "The Bakers' Broadcast." It remains a mystery to Grace. What is so funny about a man with a silly voice saying "Wanna buy a duck?" or the character in this film who is now running around his house in the middle of the night holding a ladder?

Instead she watches the people laughing and marvels at the very fact of her being at the movies with Bud Wheeler of all people. She usually spends Saturday evenings at home reading library books or listening to music. When she told her father tonight that she was going to the movies, he gave her an odd sidelong glance but said nothing. He was sitting in his armchair by the radio, a pale moody figure in shirtsleeves and vest. Yesterday she told him about the house on Queen Street. She had prepared herself for a difficult scene, expecting him to be angry for not consulting him. Instead he surprised her by observing that with banks now paying such a low return on deposits, property was probably a good place to put her aunt's legacy. Its value could only increase when times got better. As he offered these remarks, Grace realized that her father was assuming that she would be renting the house on Queen Street. Then and there she decided that she would wait a few days before telling him that she planned to live in it. People need time to get used to new ideas; just telling him that she had bought the house was a good first step.

After the movie Grace and Buddy stand outside the Capitol Theatre. Buddy asks her if she would like to go dancing at the Blue Room. This invitation is offered in his habitual joking manner, for he already knows the answer. He can't picture Grace Stewart drinking gin and orange from a bottle under the table, or dancing to saxophone music. Besides, he doesn't have money for the Blue Room. He then suggests that they go to the Royal Café for coffee and pie. But she wants to be away from people. She wants to be alone with him on this warm damp evening. To walk under the leaves of the trees along Queen Street and watch the darkness fall across the town. Most of all, she wants to show him her house. When she tells him this, he is both amused and impressed.

"No kidding! You own a house, Gracie?"

Five minutes later they climb out of the old Ford and he stands looking at her house.

"You really own this, Gracie? Boy, that is really something!"

She smiles at his incredulity.

"Let me show you around," she says.

She wonders about the propriety of escorting a young man into an empty house at this time of the evening. Her new neighbours will be watching from behind curtains, and so once inside she turns on lights as she enters each room. The bare hardwood floors creak under their footsteps as he follows her through the house.

"As you can see, it needs work," she says to him. "I'll have to put new wallpaper in all these rooms."

As she shows him around, she can't help wondering whether Buddy Wheeler is handy; she can see him helping her to paste the long sheets of paper to these walls. It's a cumbersome job that she has watched her father do many times over the years. For a moment they stand in the bathroom staring at the immense claw-footed tub. It could easily fit two, thinks Buddy. He follows her down to the kitchen and then along the narrow steps to the basement to inspect the furnace and coal bin and fruit cellar. Why, he wonders, does she want such a big house?

The whole experience is somewhat unsettling for him, and as he follows her around with his hands in his pockets, he tries to sort things out. Grace Stewart is only his age and yet she owns a house that is much better than his father's. It seems somehow unreasonable and unfair, but maybe not. It depends on how you look at these things. The house he was born and raised in is nothing more than an unpainted frame box with a sagging back porch. When the wind is easterly, you can smell the coal dust from the shunting engines along the tracks by the bay. The yard is cluttered with chicken coops and piles of weathered lumber for projects his father never even gets around to beginning. By the side of the house is a rusted-out Ford truck without wheels. It's been there as long as Buddy can remember; he played in it as a child. And of course there is the privy at the back of the yard where they do their business. Not like the bathroom in this house where you have all the privacy you could ask for. In his house they take turns having a wash in the laundry tub in the kitchen. When he was fifteen or sixteen and his sisters were all at home, he knew they were looking at his thing when he had his Saturday night bath. He used to look at them too. Shameful in a way. In his house you can hear a fart in the next room. And here was all this space for one person!

On the veranda Buddy watches Grace turn the key to lock the front door. It is a night for toads on the sidewalk and mosquitoes in the air and Buddy slaps one on his neck. He tries to measure Grace Stewart's early success and his obvious lack of it. She owns a house and has a steady job teaching school. Maybe her father bought the house for her, but so what? The point is she owns it, while he owns nothing. The clothes on his back, another pair of trousers and a sports jacket, two hockey sticks, his skates, a first baseman's mitt. It was pitiful when you thought about it, which in fact he hasn't done until this evening. As they walk to the car, Buddy takes her large, dry hand.

"You've seen me play ball now, Gracie, but softball is nothing. It's just something to do in the summer. You should come and see me play hockey. That's really my game. Hockey is . . ."

He is suddenly shy and uncertain about his ability to

describe his love for the game. Maybe this kind of love can't be described to someone who has never played hockey. How can he tell her what it feels like to skate onto fresh ice? Or the feeling you get when the goaltender doesn't even move on your shot. All you see is the light going on and the crowd rising behind the mesh as you round the net. How can you tell a woman what that feels like?

"Hockey," says Buddy, "is what I know I can do really well. It's something I'm good at, Gracie. I hope you don't think I'm a braggart, because I don't mean to be."

Grace gives him that sidelong glance she has inherited from her father. It is a look reserved for all peculiar statements and is meant to convey an ingrained skepticism. *You can't be serious!*

"But do you get paid for playing that game?" she asks.

The idea of it strikes her as preposterous. She has seen children playing the game on winter streets with a piece of horse dropping, and in January, Mr. Olson, the school's janitor, waters a patch of snow and turns it into an ice rink where the grade seven and eight boys play hockey. But she associates the game entirely with childhood; like sledding or skipping rope, it is something you put aside as you grow older.

"I don't get money for it," Buddy says. "Well, sometimes we get expenses. Supper money when we're out of town. A few dollars here and there."

He confesses this quickly as though ashamed; already he can sense her disbelief in the worth of doing something for so little.

"But the team is getting a new owner," he continues. "A man named Fowler. He's taken over McKay Motors on Bay Street and he's bought a piece of the Huron House with Leo Kennedy. Didn't you read the piece Chip McNeil wrote about him in the paper?"

Under the street lamps with the broad covers that look like Spanish hats, her face is thoughtful and grave.

"I don't read the sports page as a rule," she says.

Above them moths dance in the wide circle of light.

"Mr. Fowler is from up near Ottawa," says Buddy. "He is supposed to be a friend of T. P. Gorman. Do you know who he is, Gracie?"

She offers him a shy resigned smile.

"Come on, Gracie," he says, "you're a schoolteacher. Don't your kids tell you anything? T. P. Gorman was the coach of the Chicago Black Hawks last year. They won the Stanley Cup. And now he's back in Montreal and is going to manage the Maroons. And this Mr. Fowler is a friend of his. He's going to operate our team. We're going to have new sweaters and all kinds of stuff."

When Buddy first heard all this, he was tremendously excited. But now, under Grace Stewart's inquiring gaze, he feels somehow depleted. It no longer seems like such a swell thing! And why for that matter should a grown man get so worked up over a new hockey sweater? It doesn't make a helluva lot of sense. And it all could be just talk anyway! And talk is cheap, but whisky costs money, as his father says. Leaning on the car he looks again at the house.

"That's some place you got there. You going to rent it?" There is now almost a hint of reproach in his voice, and he has withdrawn his hand.

"No," she says, "I'm going to live in it."

Again he looks at her under the streetlight, impressed by her air of quiet determination.

"Why? Don't you live with your father?"

"I want to be on my own." She utters this simple declaration without rancour or self-pity. Buddy shrugs.

"I guess that would be nice all right."

He can see her moving around inside all that space. Taking a bath in that eight-foot tub!

"How are you going to look after a big house like that? Things can go wrong with a house."

She makes no reply and he immediately feels sorry for having sounded so mean in the face of her good fortune. He takes her hand again, and she feels a small current of pleasure running up her arm and along her spine.

"You'll need a man around the place, Gracie," he says grinning.

To his surprise she smiles at this. "I might," she says.

She is happy with Buddy Wheeler holding her hand under this street lamp in front of her house. She looks up at the circle of light and the darting moths. No one has touched her since she was ten years old and a boy named Elliot Summers kissed her on the cheek at a birthday party for a neighbour's child. But happiness for Grace Stewart does not arrive without the presence of its evil stepsisters, uncertainty and doubt. They stand by the doorway to cast their shadows over any notion that happiness in this life is unconditional and gratis. You have to pay for everything. This she knows in her heart's blood. Buddy Wheeler, for example, is agreeable company and stirs within her a mysterious pleasant longing. But he also drinks. The smell of those comfits on his breath is as sure a sign as any. Grace can remember a Mr. Dale who worked with her father. When he came to the house, he would conceal the evidence of his habit with sen sens. Grace's mother used often to remark on it and issue her warning to all mankind: "Beware the drinker, for he will bring your house and all within its walls to ruin." Common knowledge. Yet people can often be persuaded to change their habits. Did she really believe that or just want to believe it? I wonder. In any case, before they part on this evening, they agree to "another outing," as Grace puts it. It will be a picnic next day at Little Lake Park and she will provide the food. Buddy says he will take her for a boat ride.

PETTINGER'S MANUSCRIPT ARRIVED this afternoon and Linda was right. It *is* a monster: two boxes, each of which once held five hundred sheets of white bond paper, but now are filled with a thousand pages of words. All those consonants and vowels arranged in such a manner so that order and meaning emerge out of chaos. Or so one hopes. One human being's imaginative vision fashioned into language. A mystery how it's done. I've marvelled over it all these years. Pettinger, it seems, eschews the word processor; I can recognize the typescript from an old IBM Selectric. The stenographers and secretaries at Caedmon House had those bulky, grey machines on their desks when I first went to work there as a sales representative in the early sixties. It will take a great deal of reading to get through this, and yet I am inspirited beyond telling by the prospect. Charles Pettinger's manuscript at last! Twenty years' labour in two boxes of typewriter paper! I think of all the letters poor Del Shannon wrote during those years. And now here is the novel on the dining-room table before me. It must have been a great disappointment to Del not to have seen this through to publication, though he never mentioned it when I would visit him at Casey House. Perhaps we do not dwell on the disappointments in our lives when we are dying.

I have this harmless compulsion about starting things in the middle of the day; it must be first thing in the morning for me, I'm afraid. And so I was putting the manuscript aside for work tomorrow when the phone rang. When I picked up the receiver, I heard my daughter's voice. Dutiful child, she phones once a week to see how I am getting on. Brenda is in her twenties and single, a lawyer in Vancouver. All my family has lived on the West Coast for the past twenty years. My son Bradley hardly ever calls, but Brenda, in her own way, is affectionate and full of regard for the old pater. Like her mother, she is tough as iron, and I would hate to be on the other side of her in the courtroom. She is always a little brisk and bossy with me but she means well.

"How are you, Dad? How are you feeling?"

"I'm all right. I'm getting there, I think."

"Have you sold Grandma's house yet?"

"No, but Mrs. Chernyk is working on it."

"How is the Hungarian lady anyway?" asks Brenda. "Is she still wearing that outfit?"

I had told her about Mrs. Chernyk and her canary-coloured pantsuit. Brenda gets a kick out of such things; there is a mildly satirical side to her.

"What have you heard from your employer?" she asks. "Are they still paying your salary?"

Brenda can't help cross-examining you even in casual conversation.

"Yes," I say, "so far. I received my cheque today as a matter of fact."

"Don't let them screw you, Dad. You put thirty years into that place. Don't let them con you into some kind of severance package unless you get the deal you deserve. Wrongful dismissal suits are big business these days. You can sue their asses off."

I still can't get used to the casual profanity that Brenda's generation casts into conversations. They often sound like stevedores.

"Is that Linda what's-her-face giving you a hard time?"

"Linda Macklin."

"Don't take any shit from her, Dad! You don't have to after thirty years. I know a couple of good people in Toronto who specialize in this kind of thing. I can give you their names if you like."

"Brenda, you already have me in court when in fact there is no need for such measures at this point in time, as they say nowadays. As far as I know, I am still in the business. They even sent me a manuscript to read today. Charles Pettinger's long-awaited novel. That phrase will probably go on the dust jacket. Anyway, it's here on your grandmother's dining-room table! You must recall Pettinger's name? Everybody was reading him twenty or so years ago . . ."

I should know better. Brenda has already tuned out. She isn't interested in the kind of book I'm talking about. When she reads something other than briefs or transcripts, it is usually historical. Her bookshelves contain these enormous volumes that deal with war among Lombardy princes in the thirteenth century or the rise of Tudor England. She has not inherited my love for words; she regards them only as conveyors of facts or as weapons to be used against an adversary in law. Three thousand miles from her office, I can sense her impatience with my prattling on about literature.

"Have you seen your mother or Bradley lately?"

"Last Sunday for dinner," she says. "I took the early ferry over. Made a day of it. They never come to see me."

"And how are they?"

"Mother is about the same. Bradley is his usual tiresome self. If I hear another word about logging on the island . . ."

It is true. Bradley is a tiresome scold, filled to the brim with all the correct sentiments and ever eager to remind you, as if anyone in this century needed reminding, of our human tendencies to greed and self-destruction. Bradley is a busy participant in rallies and protest marches with a closetful of T-shirts espousing various causes. His high-mindedness is laudable enough, I suppose, but he irritates me with his proselytizing and his refusal to abandon childish habits. He still leaves lights burning in rooms and scrapes half his dinner into the garbage pail. A year younger than Brenda, he lives at home with his mother and works at a day-care centre.

He has always been his mother's boy, and in some ways he reminds me of myself when younger, though I was always made to turn out lights and eat what was placed before me. I was doubtless too harsh with Bradley when he was small.

A bad father. Even now, on the rare occasions when we meet, it takes only fifteen minutes before I must resist the urge to shout at him. I know I am being unreasonable, but I can do nothing about it. Inconsequential things he does and says still get under my skin. He uses, for example, the term "a tad" to mean "a little." "We need a tad more awareness about the plight of whales." It drives me wild.

Last year I visited my estranged family in British Columbia. I stayed with Brenda in Vancouver and travelled over to Victoria to see my son and ex-wife. Gillian has done well for herself out there; she owns a travel agency. Looking at her I can still see the crisply handsome English girl who used to serve drinks aboard DC-8s. Her hair is now grey and cut short. She dresses very smartly and looks altogether successful. These days Gillian and I are distantly polite to each other, neither forgetting nor forgiving the differences that separated us, yet recognizing all the same the need to maintain civility. Our wrangling days are behind us and we have established a kind of wry truce. Because of our son and daughter, we see one another once or twice a year and that is just about right.

Last year I borrowed Brenda's car and went across to Vancouver Island on the ferry. I was to pick up Bradley and take him home and the three of us would then go out to dinner. At Merrymaker's Day-care Centre, they told me that Bradley and Dawn had taken the children to the public library for story hour and so I waited in the car. After half an hour, I saw Bradley turn the corner at the head of a line of little children who were kept in tow by means of a rope which each child grasped. A young blond-haired woman in jeans took up the rear. As my son passed me on the other side of the street, I felt a pang of remorse for my failure to love him more completely and uncritically. He is overweight, he wears his hair in a ponytail, and he has an earring. In many ways he still looks like an overgrown replica of the child who used to plug the toilet and run weeping from my anger to his mother.

I ask my daughter when I can expect a visit from her.

Brenda says, "I don't know, Dad. I was thinking about Christmas."

"That would be fine," I say. "How is Chad by the way?"

Chad is the latest young man in her life.

"He's all right."

She doesn't elaborate, but from the pallid tone of her voice, I sense that Chad's days may be numbered.

I belong to a generation that is mindful of the cost of long-distance calls even when they are being paid for by someone else. I can't get used to the idea of spending money for words that disappear into air. My son and daughter, on the other hand, have no difficulty with this. Nor did their mother. It was a source of disagreement between us. Gillian used to talk to her parents in England once a week while I stood fretting. It was silly in a way, but I couldn't help scolding her for this.

"You're just checking in, Gill," I would say. "You're just making sure everything is fine over there. You don't need to ask about the weather. Who cares about the weather? The bloody weather will only change tomorrow."

I had picked up the word "bloody" from her. During these lectures Gillian's pale English face would brighten with anger. Two pink spots would appear across her cheekbones.

"Don't be absurd, Howard!" she would say. "Why do you begrudge me a weekly phone call to my parents?"

"But you talk for half an hour about the bloody weather."

"Rubbish." And so on . . .

I think about this as I listen to Brenda warn me again to watch my step.

"Remember what I said, Dad. This Macklin bitch sounds tough. If you need help, let me know."

"I feel secure and protected having a daughter like you."

"Don't be cute, Dad! You know damn well you can be pushed around. Mother used to push you around."

"Maybe so. It was a long time ago."

"Yeah, but I remember."

There is always an awkward moment before Brenda and I part company on these calls. Neither of us knows quite how to say goodbye to the other; we are both wary of sentiment. Usually an ironic stance works best for us.

"Keep in touch, daughter," I say.

"I will, father. Take care."

"Yes."

ONE FRIDAY AFTERNOON in October 1954, I visited my father in his room at the New American Hotel on Roncesvalles Avenue in Toronto. I hadn't seen him for nine years; he was a memory, a household ghost, a reminder, if ever I needed it, of the perils that await the irresponsible, of the fate in store for those who indulge their fancies and fail to keep their noses to the grindstone and shoulders to the wheel. As a child you either rebel or cower in the face of such cautionary tales. Unfortunately, I cowered and grew into a solemn and rather cautious young man who worked hard in school and pleased his mother.

The day before that Friday in October 1954, my mother and I had driven down from Huron Falls in her sturdy little prewar Dodge coupe to set me up at university. I was nineteen years old and eager to be away. I had wanted to come down alone to register, but Mother would have none of that. And so, as we stood in line at the University Housing Agency on St. George Street, I had to endure the pitying glances of those who were making their own arrangements for accommodation. I suppose my face was flushed as we shuffled forward in the long line to consult the listings for boarding houses and rooms.

We looked at several places in the Bloor and Huron street district. On the second and third floors of these Victorian brick houses, young men and women were unpacking clothes and phonographs; others were pinning to the walls of their rooms those triangular cloth pennants that were bought as souvenirs to announce that one had visited a particular city or supported a certain team. In one house a girl came out of the bathroom in a housecoat, her head enwrapped in a turban that had been fashioned from a towel. Her feet were in furry slippers and she smelled of bath oil. It had never entered my mind that university life might include living next door to a girl and sharing the bathroom with her. It may, however, have entered Mother's because in the end she chose Mrs. Leckie's for me.

It was a tall, narrow brick house on Washington Avenue. I learned much later that the poet Margaret Avison lived just down the street. The house was owned by an elderly Scots widow who had two rooms to let. One was already occupied by a gaunt young man who looked very like the pianist Glenn Gould; in that time of crew cuts he wore his hair unfashionably long about the neck. He passed like a shadow in the hallway while we were being shown the room. Three or four years older than I, he seemed frighteningly intense. As I discovered, he was a fourth-year philosophy student studying the work of Ludwig Wittgenstein. His parents were in the diplomatic service and lived abroad. He had been at Mrs. Leckie's, summer and winter, for three years. This young man would eventually achieve some eminence in the academic world but at the cost of his reason; years later a friend of mine in the publishing business, who had been trying to get a book from the philosopher, told me that he had been permanently confined to an institution.

At Mrs. Leckie's there was also a large tortoiseshell cat, an animal that seemed to embody the stealth and silence of that house where often the only sound was the ticking of the grandfather clock in the front hallway. Each night before she retired, Mrs. Leckie would insert an enormous brass key into the entrails of the clock and there would emerge a ratchet-like noise that signalled the end of another day in our existence.

Mrs. Leckie and my mother saw in each other kindred spirits who had subdued a feckless male world and had remained vigilant against the snares and pitfalls of this earthly life. I remember sitting on the narrow bed in my room looking out the window at Mrs. Leckie's cat as it crouched in the grass awaiting a sparrow. I could hear the murmur of voices from the hallway below, and I moved soundlessly to the head of the stairs. Mother was sitting at a desk near the front door affixing her bold, handsome signature to a series of postdated cheques. Her voice carried up the stairwell.

"Howard is a good boy, Mrs. Leckie. He will give you no trouble."

"I'm sure of that, Mrs. Wheeler," replied Mrs. Leckie.

And of course they were both right. I wasn't the sort of young man to give anyone trouble.

When my mother drove away (after further instruction on the management of my allowance), I was, like countless others in such circumstances, both happy and fearful. For the first time in my life I was now, more or less, on my own. And I was glad to be away from Mother. No doubt she inherited a bossy streak from her father, but her relentless need to control others also had something to do, I suspect, with her profession. Teachers, by and large, are terrible know-it-alls as you will discover if you meet them socially. After years in the classroom, surrounded by youngsters who know less and require correction, many teachers assume a spurious authority; they take it for granted that most people need to be told things, and that it is their task in life to do the telling.

During adolescence, I had quietly submitted to Mother's rule, turning along the way into a sullen youth who had inherited none of his father's athletic prowess. In high school I took refuge in books: a dull, laborious fellow whose only friend (and this was in my final year) was the sardonically witty daughter of one of the town's three physicians. In our last year at Huron Falls District High School, Liz Craig and I formed an alliance that was based not so much on affection as on mutual contempt for those around us. We were an exclusive club of two members who thought that our classmates and teachers and indeed the citizenry of Huron Falls were hopelessly mired in rusticity. Liz and I shared an interest in Somerset Maugham's *Of Human Bondage* and in a mildly salacious game involving book titles and authors, the mere mention of which could send us both into hysterical laughter. *The Open Kimono* by Seymour Hair. *The Cat's Revenge* by Claude Balls.

For the last month of our high school lives, we participated in an odd and rather touching little ritual that spoke to our romantic yearnings. Rising in the dark we stole from our houses and met at the entrance to the park. There we made our way through the trees to the edge of the lake to await the dawn. As the sky brightened and the birds began to sing, Liz and I watched for the sun that arose through the trees across the lake to flood our world with light. At that moment we recited a poem that Liz had learned at summer camp.

> Listen to the salutation of the Dawn!
> Look to this day!
> For it is Life, the very Life of Life.
> In its brief Course lie all the
> Varieties and Realities of your Existence:
> The Bliss of Growth,
> The Glory of Action,
> The Splendour of Beauty;
> For Yesterday is but a Dream
> And Tomorrow is only a Vision;
> But Today well lived makes
> Every Yesterday a Dream of Happiness
> And every Tomorrow a Vision of Hope
> Look well therefore to this Day!
> Such is the Salutation of the Dawn!

With our hearts strengthened by the transient beauty of the sunrise and the sonorous power of all those capitalized words (*the very Life of Life*), we returned to our homes for an hour's sleep and another day among the unwashed. Oddly enough my mother never discovered these early morning excursions. I mention these minor details of my life to give you some idea of the peculiar young man I was when I encountered my father for the first time in nine years.

On that Thursday evening in October 1954 bolder youths might have seized their moment of liberation and sought the company of other fellows to drink beer and chase girls. I went for a walk. In the soft darkness of that fall evening I walked for the first time in my life among strangers. Like a character in a novel by Balzac, I marvelled as I walked along the leaf-strewn streets at my escape from the country and my aloneness in the city. There were parties in progress. Along St. George Street the big fraternity houses were ablaze with light and I could see young men and women holding glasses of beer and leaning into one another by windows. There was laughter and piano music. But like many on their first evening in a strange city, I ended up at a movie house. The film was John Huston's *African Queen*. It was going around for the second time as part of a double bill, and I sat in the darkened theatre watching Humphrey Bogart, as the drunken ne'er-do-well Charlie Allnutt, manoeuvre his steamboat down a river in Africa while being bossed around by the pious spinster Katharine Hepburn. The Bogart character is a Canadian and watching him put me in mind of my father. In middle age did he too now look like this unshaven wreck who drank Gordon's gin straight from the bottle? Was he also capable of the same kind of restoration that Bogart undergoes at the hands of Miss Hepburn? I knew that my father was now living in Toronto after several years "out east." I had heard my mother tell Mrs. Parker that "Ross is now in Toronto living with some woman in a hotel on Roncesvalles Avenue." How on earth she discovered this I will never understand, but she always seemed to know of his whereabouts.

Much of that night I lay awake listening to Mrs. Leckie's dreadful clock and thinking about my father, willing myself to undertake an adventure that my timid nature was ill-suited for. Still by the following afternoon I found myself on a streetcar westbound along Queen to Roncesvalles Avenue, staring out the open window at the bright sunlight and the busy, shabby street. In those days west Queen Street was filled with immigrants. There were old women in black, kerchiefs on their heads, and middle-aged men in long leather coats and fedoras. Clusters of these newcomers from Europe stood by the windows of appliance stores and stared at television sets while I, a modern Telemachus in search of Odysseus, gaped at them and wondered what I would say to my father when we met.

As it turned out, the first hotel I entered was the New American near the corner of King and Roncesvalles. In the stale dry air of the lobby I breathed deeply and asked the clerk if someone named Buddy Wheeler lived there. The clerk, a thin, sallow fellow with a pencil moustache (the very picture of a seedy hotel clerk: a reformed alcoholic or a man on the run from an angry wife) was reading a Mickey Spillane novel. He didn't seem in the least surprised by my question. Without looking up he said, "I don't know if he's in right now," and my heart quickened. My father was actually living in this place! I stood there saying nothing and perhaps it was my helpless innocent air, but the clerk looked up from his paperback and after appraising me said, "I'll have a look in the bar for you."

Putting down the book he arose and walked to a door and opened it. At once I heard the voices and laughter and glimpsed men drinking and a white-shirted waiter bearing a tray of glasses. I could smell the beer and cigarette smoke from what in Ontario used to be called a beverage room: a place where hopelessly lost souls spent their afternoons drinking draft beer. Or so I was brought up to believe whenever my mother mentioned the patrons of the Huron House. When the door closed, I stared at the lurid cover of the detective novel and at the Maple Leaf Gardens calendar on the wall above the desk.

Then a woman walked into the lobby and entered the tiny elevator. She was somewhere in her thirties, tough and sexy-looking, wearing one of those imitation leopard skin coats with matching high-heeled shoes. She had extraordinary legs. Before pressing the button that closed the elevator door, the woman looked at me with defiance and hostility. When the clerk returned he shrugged.

"He might be in his room. Two fifteen."

I hesitated. "Can I go up and see?"

He smirked at me. "Are you a tough guy or something? Does Bud owe you money?"

At first I didn't get the sarcasm in his voice.

"No. You see . . ." I began.

Dismissing me with a wave of his hand he said, "Up the stairs, kid. Second floor. Two fifteen."

He doesn't even have a telephone in his room, I thought as I climbed the stairs. On the second floor a maid pushed a cart of towels and sheets along the hall, and from a room came the voice of Hank Williams singing "Your Cheatin' Heart." The hockey calendar, the beer parlour, the frayed little man behind the front desk, the tough-looking woman, the worn burgundy carpet, the sentimental country music: it was exactly the kind of place I imagined my father or the Humphrey Bogart character living in before they are rescued by the forces of goodness. At room 215 I stopped and listened to Hank Williams' warning of the inevitable sadness surrounding infidelity.

There was no sound from the other side of my father's door, and I almost hoped he wasn't in. Perhaps he was in bed with this "woman" my mother had mentioned. I thought of slipping a note under the door. But what could such a note say? "Long time, no see. How are you? Your son, Howard."

What words could begin to fill the space of all those years after he decided that he could no longer abide by the rules that govern the lives of most men? What could I say to a father who had cast himself adrift to live in hotel rooms and eat his breakfasts in restaurants? He had left his home and wife and child and never returned. Since then a war had been fought and won. Atomic bombs had been exploded. Automobiles were now longer and sleeker and households had refrigerators and television sets. There were thousands of people in the country who could not speak a word of English. And I was no longer a ten-year-old boy in sweater and short pants, but a gawky nineteen-year-old about to start his life away from his home and his mother.

Then the door opened and he stood before me. I was now as tall as he was. He stood there in dark trousers and a white shirt with the French cuffs rolled back over his forearms. His dark blond hair was now streaked with grey and tousled. One side of his face was creased with sleep. And God help me, I was as judgemental as Mother would have been had she seen him like this. Could there be any hope in this world for a man who is sleeping at three o'clock on a Friday afternoon? He was gaunt but still handsome in his early forties. I caught a whiff of the sleeper's sour breath. But what I remember most was that my father stood before me in his stocking feet and a man is always more vulnerable unshod. Worse, he had a hole in one of his socks and a white toe protruded. I was utterly crestfallen by the sight of that bare white toe.

When my father sold cars for George Fowler, he was careful about his clothes, but his shoes came in for special attention. He favoured heavy pebbled Florsheim brogues which he bought at Sanderson's Shoes alongside doctors and bank managers. In summer he sported white-and-tan loafers. Now he stood before me, a tired-looking middle-aged man with a hole in his sock and a baffled expression on his face. When he uttered my name, it took the form of a question.

"Howie?"

I think I said, "Yes, it's me."

Buddy Wheeler was one of those men who retain a boyishness in dress and manner and expression, so now I heard him say, "Well, for crying out loud! Come in! Come in!"

He stepped aside and I entered the small bare room with its dresser and closet and bed and chair. The sports section of the *Telegram* lay on the unmade bed and clothes were scattered about. My own room at Mrs. Leckie's was tidier. There was a washstand and a mirror, but he obviously had to go down the hall to go to the toilet. I pictured him half asleep in his pyjamas returning to this room at three o'clock in the morning to the sound of water moving through old pipes in the walls. My father looked nervous and wary. Well, it was a surprise! Nine years pass and suddenly your own flesh and blood appears on your doorstep. And for what? To reproach you? To remind you of another life that was lived in your absence? He offered me a shy grin.

"What brings you to the city, Howie?"

Had I come to this dreary hotel to punish him? We punish such people by recounting our accomplishments.

"I'm going to university," I said. "I start on Monday."

He nodded his head, eager to please.

"No kidding? University? But that's great. Just great."

He didn't ask what I was going to study, but waved me to a wooden chair by the window. A waiting-room chair. The kind you used to see at the dentist's or outside the principal's door. I imagined the management of the New American Hotel buying a hundred of these chairs at a fire sale and placing one in each room. And hopeless, romantic young man that I was, I saw my father sitting on this chair in the fading evening light, looking across the streetcar tracks to Lake Ontario, and feeling penitent when he thought of Huron Falls and the wife and son he had abandoned. Now he was perched on the edge of the bed, sitting bolt upright as though the mattress were filled with thorns.

"I'm going to study English and history," I said.

He smiled. "Uh huh! That's really great."

I stared out the window at the October sun. It was now a deep red and sinking, burnishing the lake with light. From the half-opened window came the heavy, grating sound of the streetcars as their wheels rolled over the tracks. Their bells clanged. I felt excited to be in the city.

"I think I'm going to be a teacher," I said.

Very few at that age want to be teachers. Why would they? They have just left high schools where many of the people teaching them had no business being there. But like most teenagers, I had no idea what I wanted to do with my life, and so it was Mother who had suggested teaching.

"It's steady, Howard," she said. "You can always fall back on teaching." How many people have wasted their lives and bored generations of schoolchildren by heeding such counsel?

"Runs in the family, huh?" said my father. He paused. "How is your mother, anyway?"

"She's fine," I said.

There was really nothing more to say about her. She seldom mentioned his name. There were no greetings or good wishes to pass along. She had obliterated him from our lives, and I think he sensed this terrible cancelling power that she possessed. In that room in the New American Hotel we both began to feel the onset of anxiety. My father remained alert and watchful on his bed of thorns amid the scattered newspapers, while I looked out the window at the lake and the distant glowing sky. All this time I had been wondering about the woman, my mother's words burning through my brain: "Ross is living with some woman in a hotel on Roncesvalles Avenue in Toronto."

But where was the woman? For the past couple of years my head had been filled with various sordid images: a woman who looked like Joan Crawford, or one of my favourite actresses at the time, Gloria Grahame, standing in a slip, pouring a glass of whisky. An overflowing ashtray. The smell of cheap perfume. All the melodramatic baggage from movies I had grown up on. But here was only a tired, frail-looking man who had fallen asleep reading the newspaper. He appeared to live alone in a small room. Where was the harm in that? I too now lived in a small room. While mother lived in her big house on Queen Street. We were both out of her life, and she was alone again as perhaps she had longed to be for some time.

As if on cue, the woman walked into my father's room without knocking. It was, of course, the woman with the spectacular legs in the fake leopard skin coat. Now she wore a skirt and sweater with the leopard skin shoes. My father sprang to his feet.

"Lois!" he cried. "Look who's here? This is Howie. My son."

Was there a strange and unfamiliar taste to those words on his tongue? I thought so at the time. There seemed to me no suggestion of "I've told you so much about him." There was no hint that he had ever notified her of the fact of my existence. And I realized with a sudden and terrible clarity the burden we place on others by these surprise visits.

The woman looked at me and nodded. She seemed aggrieved and resentful of my presence; one of those quarrelsome women who take offence easily and are capable at a moment's notice of hurling dinnerware across a room. There was tension between them and it struck me that I had blundered into their lives at the precise moment when there was some unresolved dispute in the air.

"Howie?" my father said. "This is Lois Sparling. A friend of mine." He looked at the woman in what struck me as a pleading manner. "Howie's going to school here in the city. To the university."

Lois lit a cigarette. "That's nice," she said.

I had got to my feet as I had been taught to do in the presence of a lady. But Lois Sparling had already turned from me and picked up the newspaper from the bed. She began at once to leaf through it, squinting against the smoke. In her skirt and sweater and high heels and with the cigarette in her mouth, she looked splendidly lewd, and

I quickly sat down on the wooden chair, astonished by my priapic interest in my father's girlfriend.

"We're going out for supper," said my father. "Would you like to join us, Howie? Do you like Chinese food?"

I must have mumbled something; in fact, I had never tasted Chinese food. The sign outside the Royal Café in Huron Falls advertised "Fine Canadian and Chinese cuisine" but I had eaten only chips and gravy and bakery pie there.

"Can you hold on a bit, Howie?" asked my father. "We'll be right back."

They left and I could hear their voices trailing down the hall. There *was* some unfinished business between them and I had interrupted. Alone, I shamelessly explored my father's room. The closet held his trousers and sports jackets and one dark suit. On the rack above the hanger bar was an old Biltmore hat box. In the drawers of his dresser were shirts and socks and underclothes and a clipping from the *Telegram* announcing the death of Lionel Conacher, Canada's greatest athlete of the first half of this century. He had died during a softball game in May of that year. My father had played hockey with him in 1936. When my father came home in that spring of 1936, he brought the program from the Montreal Forum for one of the four games he played. The program lay around the house for years beneath a stack of old *Reader's Digest*s. Sometimes, on winter Sunday afternoons, I would fetch it from under the small table by the piano, and sprawled across the parlour rug, turn its yellowing pages. In the centre of the program were the line-ups for the game on Saturday, March 7, 1936, between the Montreal Maroons and the Detroit Red Wings. I can still remember many of the players' names: Young, Goodfellow, Lewis, Aurie, Barry, Conacher, Shields, Ward, Northcott, Smith. My father had been called up suddenly from Windsor and so his name was not listed. A spring housecleaning eventually claimed the old program; my mother would have been incapable of imagining that her son might one day value such a thing. I thought of her as I stood by the window in my father's room, looking down at the lights along King Street and at the dark lake beyond. At that hour she would be sitting at the kitchen table, eating her warmed-over fried potatoes with an egg and reading the *Toronto Daily Star*.

When they returned a half hour later, my father looked flushed. He was apologetic for taking so long. It was evident that they had been downstairs for drinks and this at least had put them both in better humour. My father now seemed almost playful, shaking his head and regarding me as though I were some wondrous sight to behold.

"Will you just look at this young man, Lo?" he exclaimed. "My son! And he's off to the university. Isn't that something now?"

Lois was now wearing her black and yellow coat. She was eager to be on her way.

"Let's feed him, Buddy," she said. "Let's put some food into him. He looks a little scrawny to me."

There was a hint of reproach in her hoarse smoky voice, but I realized that this was as close to goodwill as this woman was likely to muster. My father gripped me lightly at the elbow.

"Do you know something? You're right. He is too skinny. We're going to put some weight on you tonight, young fellah. You better be hungry."

We went by taxi to the Nanking Tavern on Elizabeth Street. It seemed to take forever, and I marvelled at the casual way in which my father forked over money for cab rides. We climbed the stairs to a large dining room, its walls covered with drawings of peacocks and dragons. The waiters wore white shirts and dark trousers and carried aloft enormous trays of food. Lois and my father each had a shot of rye whisky with their bottles of O'Keefe ale. He told me that Lois was from Port Colborne and worked as a cook on lake freighters. I was given to understand that she could prepare a breakfast for twelve hungry men in minutes and brook no nonsense along the way. I could believe it. My father seemed extremely proud of her, and she listened to him in wary silence, taking his compliments as her due but alert to any error in fact or interpretation. My father ordered too much food and she chided him for it. Later he would insist over my protests that I take the uneaten food with me in a large paper bag.

As the meal wore on, I began to tire of them. They talked mostly to one another about a mutual friend who had money troubles. It had something to do with horse racing. I also gathered that my father was between car-selling jobs. Money, or the lack of it, dominated their conversation and I wondered why, if money were so scarce, they spent it so prodigally on whisky and taxis and Chinese food. I was, after all, my mother's son and I lacked the charitable heart that could regard my father's extravagance that night as hospitality. Towards the end of the meal, he ordered more whisky and to my embarrassment turned maudlin. Reaching over the table he grasped my arm. There were tears in his eyes.

"I have a son at the university," he said thickly. "Isn't that something, Lo? At the university?"

Lois Sparling broke apart her fortune cookie and nodded.

"Well you and me aren't going to get there, Bud, that's for sure." She said this with an arid little smile that suggested resentment at anyone who was bound for better things. In her voice and manner was the dull flat hatred of class. But my father was either too drunk or too innocent to read these signs.

"You get all that from your mother, Howie," he said. "She was always reading books. Do you know something? When we were first married, she made up this list of famous books. Now I was never much of a reader, but she told me if I went through these books, it would be like a university education for me. She'd bring them home from the public library. I remember *Robertson Crusoe* and a book about a man in England who sold his wife to a sailor. I don't know. I couldn't finish most of them. She wanted me to write these little book reports on them. I guess she wanted to educate me. Her heart was in the right place . . ."

He shook his head, confounded by the sheer foolishness of such a venture.

"They were good books, mind you," he continued, "but

I don't know. I just couldn't stick with them." He grinned. "I just wanted to go to the movies."

And so he did! Often alone, but sometimes with me when I got older. He loved the movies with childlike wonder and he wasn't the least bit embarrassed to sit with me and three hundred other children in the Capitol Theatre on Saturday afternoon and watch *Snow White and the Seven Dwarfs* or *Pinocchio*. Now in the Nanking Tavern he was trapped by old memories.

"I liked it when your mother read to me," he said. "For about two weeks one Christmas, when you were a baby, she would read from a book about this old man living in London, England, and how he's visited by these ghosts. They change him into a better person and he starts looking after this poor family."

"*A Christmas Carol*," I said. "By Charles Dickens."

"That's the one. You'd be asleep in your crib. We'd finish dinner, and then your mother would read this story. She read well too. Of course, she was a schoolteacher. She did that for a living."

No woman likes to sit amid the ruins of a meal with the alcohol wearing off and the inevitable headache coming on and listen to a man extol the virtues, however meagre, of his wife. Who could be expected to possess such largeness of heart? Lois Sparling's brow was dark with storm clouds.

"We better shake a leg, Bud," she said. "It's getting late."

"How about one for the road?" he asked. "You want another cola, Howie? Or more of this tea?"

I shook my head and he shrugged. "I guess that's it then."

Lois Sparling left for the washroom, and my father stared at the vines and peacocks along the wall.

"Your mother," he said quietly, "wasn't like other women I knew. The first night I saw her at the ball diamond I could see that. She was wearing this white blouse and it was nearly dark. I could just see her sitting in the front row of the stands in this white blouse. The game was over and everybody was leaving. The people were standing up and moving around her, but she just sat there. She looked so still and calm, maybe refined is the word."

Another uneasy silence arose between us. I think we were now both embarrassed by this disclosure and grateful for Lois Sparling's return.

There was a mild fuss over the bill. I offered to pay my share, but my father was having none of that and waved me off. I stood by the large glass door next to the cashier and waited for them, holding the paper bag of chow mein and barbecued ribs that I would later throw in the garbage. They were still at the table figuring out the bill, each putting money down while a waiter looked on. The sight of them haggling over the bill filled me with the same kind of despair as had the hole in my father's sock that afternoon. And suddenly I wanted to be away from them, away from the disorder and aimlessness of their lives. I wanted to be back in my room at Mrs. Leckie's, listening to that damn clock and staring at the crisp new textbooks on the little desk with its gooseneck lamp. I wanted another beginning to my life.

Out on the street my father put his arm around me, his breath unearthing memories of a man returning late at night and bending over my bed. Now we stood beneath a yellow and red electric dragon on Dundas Street.

"Do you know how to get back to your place, Howie?" he asked.

"Sure," I lied.

Although I was only a few blocks away, I had no idea. A wind had arisen and it was cool now. In her thin coat Lois Sparling clung to my father's arm. The wind pressed the coat against her legs.

"You take care of yourself, Howie," said my father. "You study hard. Okay?"

"Sure," I said. "See you around."

"You bet." He punched my arm lightly and they turned away. Lois Sparling briefly looked back at me.

"Bye now," she said.

I watched them walk along Dundas Street. She was leaning into him, teetering on those high-heeled shoes. On that cool autumn night he was wearing only slacks and a sports jacket. It was the last time I saw him. I would be in England thirteen years later when he died.

MOTHER DISLIKED HAVING her picture taken. Perhaps she regarded photography as an exercise in vanity that contradicted her Presbyterian view of things. Or perhaps she just realized that she was not photogenic. She had small eyes and thin lips, but beyond those physical limitations, her photographic images all suggest a person who is impatient with the folly of this world. Even the only remaining picture of her as a child beside her father's house in a white dress and lisle stockings conveys this impression. It is a picture that seems to say, "Now, may I *please* go." And after the photograph had been taken, I see her retreating to her bedroom and her book, while a gathering of relatives murmurs below her on the veranda.

In the school pictures which are held together with rubber bands, I can watch my mother age slowly over the years. These old photographs present a melancholy record of decline for teachers. Each June they must stand in the midst of children who never grow old. Mother is always at the centre of the back row, that tall severe figure with cropped hair, staring at the camera. In the early years the boys and girls appear solemn and compliant in their striped sleeveless sweaters and short pants, their skirts and blouses and pinafores. Later the children look more prosperous and more confident. By the late sixties, the photographs are in colour and my mother's hair is grey.

Mother's best picture is a snapshot of her in a rowboat. It was taken the summer she got married. She is twenty-two and wears a white dress. She sits uneasily in the rowboat with one hand on the gunwale and the other shielding her eyes from the sun. Her face is partly in shadows, but you can tell that she is not unhappy to be where she is, and that perhaps she is a little bemused by the photographer whom I take to be my father.

The picture was taken at Little Lake Park. There, in the thirties, you could rent a rowboat for twenty-five cents an hour and transport your loved one across the shallow, reedy water of Little Lake. As you rowed, you passed older men in panama hats who were fishing for bass and perch. Mostly, however, you were alone. On the other side of the lake, you could get away from the crowded public beach on a Sunday afternoon. You could trail your hands in the clear warm water and feel the sun on your skin and forget about the cares of the week. It was an ideal place for a young couple who were still shy with one another to court. She could stare out at the large gnarled trees along the shore, yet still cast looks from time to time at the young man who was seated in front of her with his shirtsleeves rolled up. If she had trouble conversing on such an outing, the silences were made bearable by the creaking of the oarlocks and the distant cries of bathers and sea gulls.

Their courtship was swift and mysterious. During those weeks before Labour Day weekend, they must have kept mostly to themselves. She would have had no time for his friends on the softball team. She would have kept him to herself. There would have been walks in the park and rides in Joe Wheeler's old Ford that smelled of poultry feed. They had to learn to talk to one another. She must have given him reason to hope that, with her beside him, he could do better with his life. His friends and family must have been bewildered by this turn of events. What was the attraction anyway? All right, she was a schoolteacher and had a steady job, but so what? She wasn't the sort of person who would let her hair down and kick up her heels. Where could you take such a woman on Saturday night? Yet if Buddy Wheeler puzzled his friends by wooing Grace Stewart, what must she have endured? She had few friends, but she did have a father: Jim Stewart, manager of Bell and Cowle Foundry, cranky widower and paragon of community virtue. This was the man who sat next to her each Sunday morning at Knox Presbyterian Church. And it is not difficult to imagine that it was after morning worship one Sunday in July that Grace Stewart told her father about Buddy Wheeler.

She had to. You can't keep such things locked away for long in any house. Besides, she hates deception. She likes things to be "above-board," as they used to say. And so there she is on a Sunday afternoon slicing bread for egg salad sandwiches. The kitchen has a slight farty smell from the eggs and this makes her frown. She has also opened a tin of salmon and there is a small jar of pickles, a thermos of lemonade and a small chocolate cake from Mann's Bakery. She and her father finished dinner half an hour ago: cold roast pork with applesauce and boiled potatoes, raspberries and cream, tea and butter tarts from the bakery. After Sunday dinner, her father usually rests. In the winter he lies on a sofa in a large room next to the kitchen where they keep the radio, and where Grace works at her lessons during the school year. Beyond this room is a parlour reserved for rare visits from out-of-town relatives or the minister. Grace's mother was laid out in her coffin in that room, and Grace knows that one day her father will be too. She has already pictured herself in black standing by the front door receiving visitors. On the sofa her father glances at the *Star Weekly*, marking this particular account of the world's mischief with low grunts of disapproval. In the summer, he takes the various sections of the newspaper to the veranda and sits in one of the several wicker chairs that are brought out each June from the barn at the back of the property.

On this Sunday Grace hardly touched the pork and potatoes. The sight of the food had almost made her ill. Even wrapping the sandwiches and chocolate cake in wax paper has left her mildly feverish with nerves and anticipation. Now she is flushed from the heat of the afternoon which comes pouring through the screen door. A film of sweat lies across her upper lip and her armpits are damp.

She fears the odour of her own body and the imminent arrival of her father from the veranda. She longs to be alone. *Or with him.* In the cool dark hallway of her house. She sees the two of them standing in the shadows behind the coloured-glass panels of the front door, shut away from the noise and heat of the world. There will be so many things to say to him when she feels more comfortable in his company. There will be books to read. She loves to read aloud and she will teach him things that have so far passed him by. And together they can fix up the house. Working side by side. When they tire, she will make lemonade, and she will watch him drink. Watch his tanned throat as he swallows. He uses alcohol but in time she will dissuade him from the folly of such habits. To please him she will go to his softball and hockey games, but sooner or later he will have to put aside such pastimes and get a job. Perhaps in time her father can find something for him at the foundry. Yet her father worries her enormously. He will not take her news easily. An ordeal lies ahead.

When he comes into the house, he stands before her, a tall, stern man in suit trousers and white collarless shirt and suspenders. There is now a kind of mustiness surrounding him, an old man's stale smell that has seeped into his clothes and into the sofa and chairs where he reads the newspaper. The house seems infected with this odour of age and decay; you can smell it when you come in from outside, particularly on a cold winter day. This old man's odour is a source of shame to her. Now too his breath is rancid from the pork dinner. She feels a little ill inhaling the air around him. He points at the wax-paper parcels on the kitchen table.

"Are those for some kind of Sunday school picnic?"

He is searching his memory for some item from the weekly calendar of upcoming events perused not three hours ago during the sermon. The moment of truth has finally arrived, as sooner or later it must in all families. Who put the scratch on the car? Who has been into the liquor cabinet? Between parents and children the truth will out, even when the child is twenty-two.

She is now putting the food into a straw-woven picnic hamper, a quaint-looking thing she discovered behind some odds and ends in a storage room of the barn. The basket caught her fancy. It was in fact a wedding gift from distant relatives who badly misjudged the Stewarts' recreational habits, for this is the first time it has ever been used. Grace now arranges a tea towel over the food before fastening the cover.

"I'm going on a picnic, Dad," she says finally. "I'm going down to the park for the afternoon."

Her father stares at her. She can hear him breathing through the stiff hairs in his nose.

"Who are you going with?"

"His name is Ross Wheeler." She had looked up his Christian name in an old high school yearbook. Ross sounds more responsible and mature than Buddy.

"Wheeler?" says her father. "The Wheelers who live down on Dock Street?" He obviously can't believe his ears.

"Yes," she says.

"Joe Wheeler's boy? The hockey player?"

"Yes."

Jim Stewart is peering at his daughter as though seeing her for the first time in his life.

"Why?"

"Because we went to the movies together and decided to go on a picnic today."

Her father looks mildly dumbfounded. "You went to the movies with Joe Wheeler's boy?"

"Yes."

"When?"

"Last night."

"Why?"

He now strikes her as rather stupid with his staring eyes and his questions. There is a hint of impatience in her voice.

"Dad, I felt like it."

"You felt like it . . ."

Her father pauses momentarily, afraid to continue this conversation lest something truly awful will be unveiled before his eyes. For the old man, it is one of those moments that most of us endure once or twice in our lives when we are utterly flummoxed by the actions of someone we love and think we understand.

"Well, I just don't understand that at all," he says. "Where would you meet a man like that anyway?"

"A man like what?"

"Like Joe Wheeler's boy."

"What kind of man is that?"

She can now feel her face growing warm and she warns herself to be careful. This is a house where words uttered in anger can provoke weeks of silence. It is a house where people do not forgive or forget without pain.

Her father walks across the kitchen to stand by the window overlooking the garden. He gazes out at the rows of beans and tomatoes as though ashamed to face her.

"Well for heaven sakes, Grace, the Wheelers," he says at last. "Old Joe Wheeler! They live down on Dock Street. They're on relief. They take coal from the railway tracks. Joe Wheeler worked at the foundry years ago, but he drank himself right out of a job. He spends half his time drinking. They say he bootlegs too. As for those daughters of his . . ."

Jim Stewart stops, unable to bring himself on a Sunday afternoon to record the iniquities of Joe Wheeler's daughters.

"That whole crew isn't worth a bucket of coal dust," he says, turning to sit down in a rocking chair by the window. He looks, Grace thinks, old and clumsy and slow. He won't meet her eyes but stares straight ahead.

"That Wheeler boy. He doesn't have a job, does he?"

"Half the men in town don't have jobs," she says.

She wants to be away from her father now. She is going to walk down to the park and meet Ross and have a picnic luncheon and perhaps go for a boat ride.

Sitting in the rocking chair her father watches her gather up the picnic things. Finally he smacks a palm against the arm of the chair.

"Well, this is the damnedest thing." He almost never swears. "It makes no sense, Grace. Going out with someone like that. That's not the sort of fellow for you."

She wonders how many fathers and daughters have gone through these ridiculous interviews.

"He's not the sort of man for you," her father repeats, wagging his head.

Is there a man or woman alive who doesn't resent another's adverse opinion of our choice of lover? This presumption of knowledge about a part of us that is surely unknown to others?

"You don't even know him," Grace says.

There is an edge to her voice and her father looks up, meeting her eyes for the first time, assailed not so much by the tone of her voice as by her statement with its suggestion of intimacy. Grace herself is aware of the irony that she doesn't really know Buddy Wheeler either. And so we blunder on, our words interpreted in any number of ways but most often by underlying fears. Most of us are pessimists under the skin. And so "You don't even know him" suggests to Jim Stewart that his daughter does in fact know him. And in ways that are perhaps foreign to decency.

Such statements send shockwaves through the fathers of daughters who see all manner of pernicious goings-on behind their backs: the assignations in dark movie houses, the furtive kisses, the couplings in automobiles, the child born out of wedlock, the public disgrace. Even upright young women like Grace Stewart can be seduced by scoundrels, and inevitably their bare white legs will be straddled across car seats as they lie beneath sweating, grunting bootleggers' sons. For a moment the old man is dizzied by such a hateful vision.

"How many times have you seen him?" he asks.

"We went to the movies last night."

"This just can't be, Grace," he says. "You can do better than Joe Wheeler's boy."

"Can I?" asks Grace, aware that her question sounds theatrical. But in fact the whole scene strikes her as foolishly dramatic: the outraged father watching his daughter leave with her picnic basket like Little Red Riding Hood off to meet the Wolf. Her father leans forward in the rocking chair, his hands clamped to the arms.

"I don't want you seeing Joe Wheeler's boy. It's not right."

By the door Grace stops. "Why not?"

"It just isn't. That's all."

"Dad," she says, "I'm going. I'll be back in time to make your supper."

"Now listen here to me, Grace."

"I'm moving too, Dad," she says. "At the end of next month I'm moving into my own house. I'm sorry but that's the way it's going to be."

She is glad finally to have cleared the air and escaped. As she goes out, she is especially careful closing the screen door which has a taut spring at the bottom. If you release such a door too quickly, it will slam shut with the sound of a shotgun implying petulance and ill will on the part of the leave-taker. And these last few weeks with her father will have to be managed adroitly. On Park Street she walks quickly, feeling both frightened and exhilarated, conscious of having passed some kind of threshold in her life. After this Sunday, things will never be quite the same between her and her father.

Ross is late and she sits for fifteen minutes at the base of the flagpole looking across to the parking lot and the small hill behind with its beds of petunias and its border of white-washed stones spelling out "Welcome to Little Lake Park." She clasps her hands about her knees and waits for him, a young woman in a white dress with an old-fashioned picnic hamper at her feet. A hundred yards beyond her is the public beach. There are children splashing near the shore or making things in the sand. Farther out young men and women are diving and jumping off the wooden rafts. She watches the sunlight on the water and the divers' legs disappearing, their heads emerging seconds later. She can hear the screams of the girls as they are tugged into the water by boyfriends. Along the beach hundreds of bathers are lying in the sun, but she feels apart from them. She can't imagine taking off her clothes and exposing her long white body to public view in a bathing suit. Fitting a tight rubber cap around her ears and wading into the water. Such things are not for her.

Finally the old black car appears and she watches him manoeuvre it into the parking lot. He gets out and walks across the grass towards her, wearing canvas shoes without socks and tan pants with a white shirt. The sleeves are rolled up past his elbows. He is grinning and holding a small camera.

"Hello, Gracie. I guess I'm a little late. Sorry."

He looks around as though half-expecting others to be present. But who would they be? They are suddenly shy with one another.

"Would you like to eat now?" she asks.

"Sure. Why not? I can always eat."

As she spreads the tablecloth over the grass, he shows her the camera.

"My sister Martha just bought this. She's home from the city for the weekend. I'm going to take your picture, Gracie."

He is like a child with a new toy. She doesn't really want her picture taken and mildly protests, but to no avail. Standing over her, he fusses with the little Brownie while she tries to hold a pose that will seem unaffected and spontaneous. It is all futile. Instead she concentrates her gaze on his hands and bare arms. The pictures from this picnic either didn't turn out or have been lost. From that summer afternoon there remains only the photograph of Grace Stewart in the rowboat, holding on to the gunwale with one hand and shielding her eyes from the sunlight with the other.

THEY WERE MARRIED in Toronto on the last day of August. My mother made all the arrangements: letters of reference, train tickets and hotel reservations. She even bought my father's wedding suit. I heard her tell this to her elderly confidante, Mrs. Parker, one blustery winter Sunday years after my father had departed. Some children are secret listeners, miniature spies who lurk behind doorways, hoping to bring back intelligence from the adult world that will help them make sense of their own, or at least prepare them for the betrayals and deceptions that lie ahead. Such children would rather overhear two women talking in a kitchen than throw snowballs at playmates. And so was I fashioned as a small boy, stationed on the other side of doors or with an ear pressed to the hot-air grate in the upstairs hall, listening to the voices from below. And it was on one such occasion that I heard my mother tell Mrs. Parker, "I even bought his wedding suit."

My mother had lived in Toronto for a year with her aunt while attending Normal School and so she was the guiding partner in this adventure. It was she who consulted the schedules and bought the train tickets. It was she who wrote the hotel and forwarded the certified cheque which they could scarcely ignore. It was she who knew where to board the streetcar when they came out of Union Station to the noise and traffic of Front Street. My father had travelled to Lakeview and Port Edward and Huntsville to play softball and hockey. Once or twice he may have visited the "city," as people in Huron Falls then called Toronto. But it was my mother who had to point the way to the hotel where they would spend their wedding night.

They were only one of several couples being married that Friday in the small brown room at city hall. They had to wait their turn. They sat on polished oak chairs in a corridor and watched lawyers in their black gowns hurrying past with shifty-looking men in tow. Here in this unfamiliar world where authority confronted the lawless, they may themselves have felt vaguely illicit. They must have been relieved when Mrs. I. Crosley (Ida? Irma? Iris? Irene?) opened the door and called their names. What did my mother wear that afternoon? Let us suppose a dove grey suit tailored to mid-calf according to the style of the day. A small Robin Hood hat with a brooch embedded in its felt side. She carries a mauve purse and there are new shoes from Sanderson's Fine Footwear. These already hurt her large narrow feet. Beside her my father grins uneasily in his new suit, no doubt dying for a shot of Old Dominion and a glass of cold beer. In the warm grey air stirred by an overhead fan, oaths are taken. Solemn promises are made. And documents are signed and witnessed.

Afterwards they walk out onto Queen Street past mothers hurrying into Eaton's and Simpsons to buy clothes for children returning to school the following week. These harried-looking housewives with their money worries remind Grace that in a few days she will be returning to Dufferin Street Public School not as Miss Stewart, but as Mrs. Wheeler. The children will understand, but Grace expects some chilliness from Miss King and Miss Hepworth who will view the matter in an unfavourable light. They will regard her behaviour as rash and unseemly. They will also be a little envious, but they will get over everything in time as we all do. When she told Mr. Ball of her plans earlier that week, he received the news with equanimity and wished her good fortune.

As they walk along Queen Street, Buddy tells her that he wants to see Maple Leaf Gardens. He wants to see the building where the Leafs play their games. Where is it anyway? She has no idea. It has stopped raining, but the sky looks threatening and her feet ache. But she wants him to be happy on this day, and so she steps into a phone booth and looks up the address of Maple Leaf Gardens in the directory. They take a trolley north on Yonge Street to Carlton and walk east to stand in front of the large grey building that is less than three years old. He tells her about Charlie Conacher and Red Horner and Harvey Jackson, players whose names he hears on the radio every Saturday night in winter. She listens to him and nods. If, on that overcast afternoon in August 1934, anyone had told him that within two years he would in fact play a game of hockey in Maple Leaf Gardens against Conacher and Horner and Jackson, he would probably have laughed in disbelief and astonishment.

The hotel she chose is the Victoria on Yonge Street south of King. Friends of her aunt's occasionally stayed there and spoke well of the place. It was clean and respectable, and what more do you want from a hotel? She had therefore paid for a night's lodgings by certified cheque accompanied by a carefully worded letter that included the words: "My husband and I will be arriving on the afternoon of Friday, August 31." Writing the words "My husband and I" had filled her with a peculiar happiness.

They register at the front desk where the clerk has taken her letter and cheque from a file folder. He scrutinizes these documents through narrowed eyes as though suspicious of their authenticity. Grace finds his attitude provoking. The lobby is empty except for a man reading a newspaper and smoking a cigar. He is surrounded by various pieces of luggage and looks like a travelling salesman waiting for a late-afternoon train that will take him home for the Labour Day weekend. The plush sofas and armchairs in the lobby are faded and worn. The hotel itself strikes Grace as a little down at the heels; not at all what she expected for the money. She watches Buddy sign the register: Mr. and Mrs. J. R. Wheeler, 389 Queen Street, Huron Falls, Ontario.

The porter, a small, tired-looking man in his forties, carries their bags to the elevator, a kind of cage with an accordion-style door made of brass. As the elevator carries you aloft, you can see the various floors of the hotel passing before your eyes. Grace also stares at the dandruff on the porter's shoulders and at the back of his head with its greying hair and creased neck. He has spent a lifetime carrying luggage for quarters and dimes. She wonders if he has a family, or lives alone with a widowed mother, sharing the crossword puzzle and listening to the radio comedian with the silly voice on Sunday evenings.

Grace and Buddy follow the porter along the sloping hallway to a small, stuffy room at the rear of the hotel. It overlooks an alley and the bare wall of a building. There is a bed, two chairs, a dresser and a small radio that will play for an hour after you insert a quarter into a slot by the dial. The porter opens the window while Grace wonders if perhaps she hasn't been "gypped," a word her father often uses as a synonym for cheated. Buddy has gone to the bathroom and she is left to search in her purse for a quarter which she gives to the small grey man.

After he leaves, Grace stands by the half-opened window, perspiring lightly, looking down at the alley which faces a laneway behind the hotel. She can see an old bearded man, the rag-and-bone man, standing by his horse, adjusting the harness. She watches him climb aboard his wagon and lift the reins. As he disappears behind the hotel, she is reminded of just such a man who used to wander the streets of Huron Falls with his horse and cart calling out for bottles and old clothes. As a child she watched him coming to the back door, paying Grace's mother for castoffs with pennies and nickels drawn from a long black purse.

By the window Grace can hear her husband urinating.

Now she will share such personal moments with a man. She has lived alone with her father for ten years and knows something of the habits of men: their bitter tobacco smell, their hacking and spitting, the noises that emerge from various orifices. Yet now she will share even more intimate moments. He has kissed her several times and touched her breasts (though she was clothed); she was stirred and somewhat frightened by these experiences. She seemed on the verge of wanting somehow to let go. And now she will have to submit to him entirely. She is not, however, ignorant of the sexual act. She has read *What Every Woman Should Know*, a pamphlet which you had to ask for at the public library. The librarian, Miss Peters, had brought it to Grace with an air of helpful authority, her manner suggesting that this indeed is what public libraries are for: helping to educate young women in these matters. Would that more young ladies in this town made use of the literature available on this subject. None of this, of course, was uttered by Miss Peters; it was merely conveyed by her look as she handed the pamphlet to Grace at the front desk.

There were line drawings of the reproductive system. The path of the spermatozoa to the egg was diagrammed and there were illustrations of the foetus at various stages of development. The last pages contained some admonitory messages about protecting oneself against unwanted pregnancy and venereal disease. The latter portions of the tract seemed to suggest that sex was a minefield for the unwary. It told you enough, however, about the act itself, and one had only to witness the couplings of dogs on the street to get a general idea of how it was done, though, of course, humans reversed the position and faced one another.

Grace has the vaguest of childhood memories, perhaps her earliest, of lying in her bed, or maybe even in her crib, and hearing from her parents' room the creaking of bedsprings and a keening sound that might have expressed either anguish or pleasure. For years the sound had puzzled her, and then she had forgotten about it. Now she realizes that her parents must have been performing the act. And then there were the coarse boys at school. She saw them in the yard at recess teasing girls by putting a forefinger through a circle made by their other hand. The gesture stood for intercourse, she supposed, though what a nine-year-old would know about such things was difficult to imagine.

There would doubtless be some initial discomfort, though one gathered from the booklet that it could eventually become an enjoyable experience. If conception were to be avoided, the man had to withdraw his organ before ejaculation or wear one of those rubber coverings that she sometimes saw washed up along the shores of Little Lake or floating in the bay at the town dock. Had he bothered to buy any she wondered? Yet she doesn't really care. In a way she would like to get that part of her life underway. She would like two children, a boy and a girl, and already she is thinking that if she becomes pregnant, she will have the child next summer. She will inform Mr. Ball as soon as she finds out and she will work until the Easter holidays. She has money laid by in case Ross still hasn't found a job.

Next September she will again be ready to return to the classroom; she certainly doesn't intend to give up teaching. She will ask Violet Day's mother about her daughter looking after a house and baby during the week. With careful planning, these things can be made to work.

The thick humid air of the city surrounds her; it wells up from the narrow alley and enters through the half-opened window. Grace sprinkles a handkerchief with cologne and presses the cloth against her throat, thinking of the trees along Queen Street and her cool dark house and the fresh air off Georgian Bay. It would be intolerable to have to live in Toronto all summer. She has already planned the rest of the day. They will go to the Canadian National Exhibition. Her parents used to take her there every Labour Day weekend as a treat before school. She will show him the various exhibits where you can pick up free samples from the salesmen in the booths: little pots of mustard and packages of yeast, miniature boxes of cereal and chocolate bars. Nutrition posters for the classroom. They can have their supper at the Stoodleigh Restaurant and then return to the hotel. The train for Niagara Falls leaves the next morning at nine o'clock, and she has the tickets in her purse, next to her money. She wonders when she will phone her father. That should be dealt with and soon: it is vexing to have it hanging over her head like a sodden rain cloud dampening her spirits. As far as her father knows, his daughter has gone to the Exhibition by herself. She decides that tomorrow will be time enough to tell him.

When Buddy comes out of the bathroom, he is doing up

his fly buttons. He has thrown off his jacket and loosened his tie. In his trousers and vest he looks as boyishly handsome as he did on the softball diamond a few weeks ago. He offers Grace a grin that suggests sly mischief.

"Well, here we are, Gracie! An old married couple. Are we crazy or what?"

PETTINGER'S NOVEL IS a shattering disappointment. I read until two o'clock this morning, heartsick at the lifelessness of it all. It saddens me beyond telling to report that his new book is a turbid sermon on the collapse of hope in our century. The vitality and wit so evident in his two earlier books have vanished, replaced by humourless rhetoric and dire warnings about the evils of technology. His characters cannot open their mouths without delivering major statements. The book has no narrative energy; only a bleak message that translates roughly into "I told you so." And the confounded man has been working on this for nearly twenty years! Think of it if you can bear to! Twenty years!

Now he sits in his farmhouse awaiting news from the publisher. Trembling with excitement. Sick with nerves and anticipation. Dying for that treble scotch which he has forsworn these past several years on medical advice. Can anyone with a heart not wish the man well? Can anyone not suppose what is going through his mind at this moment? After twenty years of work, they have to like it. They can't just dismiss that kind of effort and dedication.

I put a large chunk of my life into this book, God damn it. Yes indeed. He and his wife have lived with this book for nearly a thousand weeks. Over the years the novel has grown into a kind of monstrously spoiled child who has come to dominate the household. It is the one thing in their lives that must be constantly petted and praised and waited upon. Tiptoed around on bad days and solicitously inquired about on good ones. If you can read the author's mood. This apparently comes with time and practice.

"How did it go today, Charles?"

"Bloody marvellous. I think this chapter really works, Jane. I'll read some of it to you after dinner. I've made a casserole."

And what chapter did he read to her that he thought was so bloody marvellous?

It was all too dismaying for words, and so after a late breakfast I fled from the house, seeking refuge downtown in Huron Falls Public Library where the people are used to me now. I am a familiar figure to Mrs. Loomis who works in the basement where they keep town records, books on local history, collections of prominent family documents, microfilm of the local newspaper — anything that can shelter under the rubric of Huronia, the Ministry of Tourism's name for this part of Ontario. The Hurons, after whom the region is named, were a tribe of Indians who once lived in these parts before they were annihilated by marauding Iroquois from New York.

Mrs. Loomis is a friendly woman in her forties. She is convinced that I am some kind of academic person from

Toronto who is writing a book on Huron Falls. She is always eager to help and treats me with the sort of good-humoured deference you might afford a gifted child who is quite hopeless when dealing with ordinary tasks. And it is true: I am, like my father, maladroit in these matters. She sets up the microfilm contraption for me, threading the stiff film through various loops and across apertures; she adjusts the light and focus knobs, and then, like a patient teacher content to leave her pupil to work unsupervised on his experiment, departs with the words, "If you need anything, just give me a shout."

I know what she means, but I wouldn't dream of shouting at the dear lady.

As I turn the little crank, the spool of film unwinds spilling words from long ago onto the lighted screen. In 1935 you could buy a Chevrolet Master Six for $854 and a cord of hardwood for $12. Someone named Ed would clean your chimney for seventy-five cents: *Call Ed. Job guaranteed.* The headline on the sports page for a Thursday in March of 1935 reads: "Wheeler Scores Three as Flyers Nip Port Edward 5-4 to Win Series." There is a picture of my father standing in his hockey gear beside the team owner and manager George W. Fowler who has his arm around my father's shoulders.

This man Fowler changed my father's life. He came to Huron Falls the summer my parents were married. He was from up around Ottawa, the grandson of one of those lumber barons who made fortunes in the previous century. Fowler, it seems, became attached to the Georgian Bay area and decided to set up in Huron Falls. In partnership with a local lawyer named Leo Kennedy, he bought the Huron House. He also took over a moribund automobile dealership on Bay Street, hanging up a salmon-coloured oval tin sign that said Fowler Motors. He filled the lot with used cars bought from dealers in Toronto. In 1935 more people were selling cars than buying them, but if they were buying them, they were looking for used ones.

George Fowler was also a sportsman, as the sons and grandsons of rich men often are. Such people own horses and hockey players and enjoy being part of a world where trading in flesh, either animal or human, can take place over a hotel luncheon. Such men are drawn to this life as is the pike to the bass. And Fowler had connections to some important people in the sporting world of his day. He was friends with T. P. Gorman, an Ottawa man and successful figure in the National Hockey League. Fowler also knew Conn Smythe in Toronto and Leo Dandurand in Montreal. When he came to Huron Falls that summer, Fowler bought the local hockey team and controlling shares in Arena Gardens. From his rooms in the Huron House, he could smoke his cigars and plan his strategy for the team. At the time the Flyers played in an intermediate league comprising Port Edward, Lakeview, Huron Falls, Huntsville and Parry Sound.

When the team began to practise that fall, George Fowler would sit behind the players' bench in his fur-collared overcoat and homburg, smoking a cigar and watching his players. Years later I used to hear my father talking about Mr. Fowler and his cigars and overcoat and homburg. He is wearing this very garb in the picture in which he has his arm around my father's shoulders. Fowler was then somewhere in his early fifties I would guess: a stocky man of medium height, an eater of steak and eggs, a teller of blue stories, a man among men in smoke-filled rooms. There is something a little proprietary and disdainful in the manner in which he embraces my father. This is a man who is used to having his way with his fellow creatures. In the meaty Rotarian face, you can still see the boarding school bully who played left guard for the football team and flicked towels at the backsides of rookies in the locker room. But whatever his failings as a human being, George Fowler had an eye for hockey talent, and in Buddy Wheeler he saw a player who may have reminded him of other swift light men on skates like Boucher and Joliat. Watching Buddy Wheeler dip and swirl among his teammates during those Sunday morning practices in October, Fowler may even have considered phoning Tommy Gorman. But Fowler wanted a championship team in his first year, and for that he needed Buddy Wheeler. He also had to bring in a player or two from beyond the league to strengthen what was already a fairly solid local team. By the end of October, a big defenceman named Red Hanna had joined the Flyers along with George Doucette, a speedy centre who had once played in the Can-Am League with Philadelphia and Providence.

That winter, while George Fowler sat behind the players' bench in his fur-collared coat and homburg, watching Red Hanna knock down opposing forwards, and the line of George Doucette, Cully Crawford and Buddy Wheeler score goals, my mother carried me within her and taught grade three pupils how to read and write and do their sums at Dufferin Street Public School. Although physically strong, she was often tired after a day in the classroom, walking along the snowy streets with a briefcase full of scribblers, arriving home to find her young husband still asleep. It was irksome. Supper was prepared and eaten in silence, the beginning of those festering silences that over the years would poison the air of our house.

My father still had no job, though there had been an offer from old Jim Stewart who was now reconciled to his daughter's choice of husband and lived alone, waiting for a grandchild, in his big house on Park Street. But my father was not keen on foundry labour. He worried about an accident: an iron pig dropping on his foot, or an injury to one of his hands. His season would be finished. There was no telling what could happen to a man in a foundry. He had talked to Mr. Fowler about it, and the owner had agreed that foundry work was not for Buddy Wheeler. Besides, there would probably be something for him at the car lot in the spring when things picked up, as they surely would. In the midst of the Depression, men like George Fowler always spoke about "things picking up" in the manner of those who are not particularly affected by hard times. "Things aren't so bad now, Bud, and they will get even better. You mark my words." When Buddy spoke to Grace about this, she studied his face and thought about George Fowler and the kind of man he was.

Meantime there were other disappointments. When my parents moved into this house, there was a great deal of work that needed doing. Rooms had to be stripped of wallpaper and redone, a cumbersome job demanding teamwork and patience. They couldn't afford to hire tradesmen and so they had to manage themselves. But Grace soon discovered that Buddy was hopeless at these things. She could drive a nail with more accuracy than he could. And like a child, he soon wearied of the simplest task; he couldn't scrape old paint from a baseboard without growing sulky. His normal good spirits would sour before her eyes, and at supper there would be excuses.

Several nights a week he was playing hockey, and so she was alone, managing somehow to fit the large unwieldy sheets of wallpaper into place. When he crawled in beside her late at night, she could smell the alcohol and tobacco smoke on him. Now and then he wanted her and she endured his quick frantic thrusts. But mostly he lay there talking about George Fowler.

"Mr. Fowler is going to do this for me." "Mr. Fowler is going to do that for me." "Mr. Fowler thinks I can play in a professional league next year."

Listening to this, Grace grew sick of the man's name. She had seen him going into the Huron House, a self-important figure and mildly sinister in her opinion. A crony of Leo Kennedy's who defends every scapegrace in town and sells Irish Sweepstake tickets on the side. They belong to a fast crowd, a *demi-monde*, that Grace has little use for and doesn't trust. Yet lying beside her unemployed young husband, she realizes that she might need George Fowler's goodwill if Buddy is to find a job. And then one night, shortly before Christmas, an opportunity arises. She and Buddy are invited to a party in Fowler's rooms at the Huron House.

Grace is now three and a half months pregnant, her tall form filling out, though she can still wear her dove grey wedding suit. Buddy too wears the suit he was married in. After pulling on galoshes and overcoats, they walk downtown in silence through a cold still night to the Huron House. Earlier that afternoon they quarrelled over a bottle of whisky on the kitchen table. When Grace arrived home from school, she found Buddy sitting in the kitchen with a big red-headed man. In front of them on the table were tumblers and a bottle of Canadian Club. There it was! A bottle of whisky on her kitchen table! It is probably difficult for most of us to comprehend the kind of outrage that such a sight would have stirred in the hearts of certain people who were raised in this province in a particular way and at a particular time. Grace had grown up in a house where alcohol was not only forbidden, but was also condemned as the very fountainhead of ruin and disgrace. Her mother had been a member of the Women's Christian Temperance Union, obdurate lifelong enemies of booze. Grace's view of the scene before her on that December afternoon probably went something like this: it is one thing to have your husband drink in arenas and hotel rooms; it is quite another to have liquor available in your own house. That this probably makes no sense to most of us nowadays is neither here nor there. These were convictions held close to the heart of women like my mother. Grace watched the big man's freck-led hand clasp the bottle and pour some whisky into a glass.

"Gracie?" said Buddy. "This is Red Hanna. He plays with me. Red once played for the Senators."

Red Hanna wagged a large forefinger at Buddy.

"A try-out, chum. Training camp. Exhibition games. Do not mislead your good lady wife."

"You played with Clancy. You told me that."

"So I did, Bud. So I did. For two exhibition games. In the year of our Lord, nineteen and twenty-eight."

Red Hanna turned to Grace and raised his glass. He had startling blue eyes.

"Ma'am," he said.

"How do you do?" she said coldly, reminding herself to be careful. Like many others, Buddy doubtless saw the Christmas season as an excuse for licence. A chance to get drunk. But this was the first time he had brought drink into the house.

"We have to go out tonight, Ross," she said.

Buddy nodded. "I know that, old girl. Red, here, is going too. We're all going. It's going to be a time."

The big red-headed man was now going through an extraordinary routine, a pantomime of someone engaged in a futile search: he looked under the table and into his armpit; he peered beyond Buddy's shoulder at the doorway to the dining room; he even arose and opened a cupboard door. He was an excellent actor, his face a study in con-trived wonder. Buddy found this performance hilarious.

"What are you doing, Red?" he laughed.

Red Hanna was still gazing past Buddy's shoulder.

"I'm looking for some guy named Ross. Have you seen him, Bud?"

This convulsed Buddy. "That's me, dope. That's my name."

Red Hanna leaned back, his hands spread across his chest, eyes wide in disbelief.

"You are Ross? You are the actual owner of that name? Oh, Ross! I am so sorry. Let me shake your hand."

He got up at once and went around the table to pump Buddy's hand. Buddy was now beside himself with laughter. Grace had seen about enough of this foolishness and turned to leave. But not before Red Hanna made an elaborate bow and added, "Nice to have met you, ma'am. Maybe sometime soon, me and the missus will have you and Ross here over for tea."

He gave Buddy a broad wink. Grace briefly regarded the man's brutal grinning face with its nicks and scars, the immense head of stiff coppery hair, itself a kind of weapon. A born bully, she decided. One of those touchy brutes who know they can get away with sarcasm and scorn. Worse for Grace, however, was the realization that this awful man was in fact more intelligent than her own husband who was still laughing at all these antics. And at that moment, a terrible sentence passed swiftly through her mind: *I married a child.*

This was her introduction to my father's world, and as he helped her out of her coat in the lobby of the Huron House on that evening in late December of 1934, she must have considered it both alien and fantastical. It was a world in which men gathered to recall games and monkeyshines played yesterday or long ago; where mythic figures, renowned for body checks or organ size, were paraded forth in the telling. It was a rough, gregarious male world of gags and practical jokes where women were mostly decorative. It was a world of play and irresponsibility. Years later my mother told me how astonished she was to overhear the conversations of hockey players in which were discussed the latest adventures of comic-strip figures like the Gumps and Moon Mullins.

Some of them ate glass and others put their hands under their arms and made farting noises. Everything was for laughs, and the object of life, or so it seemed to my mother, was never to grow up. She used to claim that many of her pupils had more sense than my father's friends. As in most of her assessments of human conduct, I think her judgement was too harsh. Many of these men had families and responsibilities, and they took care of that part of their lives. But when they got together, a kind of collective mania surfaced. I can remember big men with bellies visiting my father in the summers when I was a young child. After a few drinks, they would start in on the jokes or ask me to guess which hand held the monkey. Mother, as usual, had no patience with the frivolous side of life.

On this December evening in 1934, there is a large Christmas tree in George Fowler's apartment which is crowded with guests: the players, of course, with their wives or girlfriends, but also local businessmen and lawyers like Leo Kennedy. The sports editor of the *Huron Falls*

Times, Chip McNeil, a thin lugubrious alcoholic who bears a remarkable likeness to the comedian Buster Keaton, is there. Included among the young women is Buddy's sister Mildred. Grace is surprised by the sight of her. She remembers Mildred as a timid little creature in high school; now she is a pretty woman with soft blond curls and a bosom. She is smoking a cigarette and laughing with two young men. There is something guileless and vulnerable, an attractive humanity, about Mildred. She is a female version of her brother and not at all like Martha or Muriel who are tougher, shrewder types.

There is beer and whisky and gin and a phonograph playing Christmas carols and pop tunes. Someone is especially fond of a novelty hit called "Who's Afraid of the Big Bad Wolf?" The song is played over and over until the big man Hanna removes the record from the player and holding the disc in both hands, breaks it apart like a biscuit. No one sees fit to argue with him. The room is hot and smoky and Grace is tired; she longs to be away from here. In her own house lying in bed under blankets, looking out through the window at the branches of the bare trees and the winter sky beyond. Thinking of the life that is growing within her. Everyone in the room talks so loudly and laughs so much that she feels the onset of a headache.

She can see George Fowler making his way through the various knots of people, grasping an elbow here, trading a joke there. The squire from the manor house mingling among the tenants at Christmastide. When Fowler sees Grace, he smiles and squeezes past several people to the chesterfield where she is seated holding a glass of ginger ale. He stands in front of her, smoking a cigar and jingling the change in his wide pants, offering her a view of himself, a broad expanse of his tailored front, trousers, vest and suitcoat, a plane of blue pin-striped cloth. His flies, a foot long, are inches from her face.

"Mrs. Wheeler?" he asks smiling down at her.

Grace looks up at him. "Mr. Fowler?"

He takes a hand out of his pocket and for an instant she thinks that he is going to offer it in greeting. She nearly brings forth her own, but sees in time that he is merely using the hand to take the cigar from his mouth. It is a practised piece of business meant to convey authority.

"Haven't seen you with some of the other ladies up at the rink. What's the matter? Don't you like watching your husband play hockey?"

Grace sips her ginger ale and wishes he would move. It is infuriating to have him standing above her like this. Crowding her. A clumsy attempt at intimidation. She knows her face is flushed.

"I'm not very interested in sports."

"Is that so?" says Fowler rocking on his heels. Through the choking cigar smoke he appears to be studying her and she believes that she can read his thoughts. *What does Buddy Wheeler see in this long plain drink of water?*

"You should come and watch your husband play sometime," Fowler says. "He's a helluva hockey player. Excuse my language."

Grace says nothing to this.

"I think," Fowler continues, "I can get him a professional contract next year. What do you think of that?"

"I would be happier if you could get him a job, Mr. Fowler," says Grace.

"A job?" Fowler says. "You mean a job around town?"

"Why yes. Where else?"

"You shouldn't hold this boy back. It's Grace, isn't it?"

"Yes."

She notices that he doesn't offer his first name. But he does finally settle in beside her. She can feel the pressure of his stout thigh against her. For a few moments they both watch the party in silence. Then Fowler turns towards her, placing his arm across the back of the chesterfield.

"Buddy tells me you teach school. He's very proud to have a schoolteacher for a wife. He tells me you read books together. That's really nice."

The mockery in his voice is deliberately casual, perfected after years of treating most people with contempt. She thinks that by now he may not even be aware of this cruelty in his voice. But she is furious with Buddy for revealing intimacies of their marriage to a man like this.

"And I understand," Fowler adds, "that a little Wheeler is on the way."

Grace ignores his coyness and stares ahead. Fowler leans forward.

"When, may I ask, is the blessed event?"

The blessed event. She turns to look at Fowler's smirking face: the meaty cheeks and thick neck; his eyes are narrow through the cigar smoke. Looking at him, it occurs to her that nothing is sacred to this man. Even the birth of a child can be made to seem ridiculous and trivial. And looking at him she knows that she will never ask George Fowler for anything. She will tolerate him for her husband's sake, but she will never seek a favour from him.

"Our child is due next summer," she says.

Fowler nods. "Well, you two certainly didn't waste any time, did you?"

Her look is so corrosive that Fowler is taken aback. It's as though he realizes that he has finally gone past an acceptable boundary with this woman.

"Exactly what are you implying by that, Mr. Fowler?" Grace asks.

Implying! It wasn't a word he was used to hearing from hockey players' wives in places like Huron Falls. In any case, George Fowler has had enough of Grace Wheeler and her snotty, schoolteacher ways. He smiles at her with amused dislike.

"Oh, I wasn't implying anything, Grace," he says. "I never imply anything. I just come right out and say it."

He taps her empty glass.

"Have another toddy and enjoy yourself! And come up to the arena sometime and watch your husband play. He's a crackerjack. I'll bet you he is playing professionally this time next year." He pauses to examine the end of his cigar. "Be a shame to hold a talented boy like that back."

Grace watches the chunky figure disappear among the couples now dancing in the middle of the room. She has made an important enemy tonight; she can feel it in her bones. Buddy is now dancing with Mildred, brother and sister executing a smart little foxtrot to the tune of "Isle of Capri." They are graceful and lithesome together, a pleasure to watch and Grace feels a surge of tenderness for her young husband. Now and again Red Hanna interrupts Mildred and Buddy and introduces him to others. "This is Ross. Have you fellows met Ross?"

In a corner of the room a big, dark-haired young man named Leo Fournier is about to perform a trick. A crowd has gathered to watch. Fournier is lying on the floor with a glass of beer on his forehead. He has wagered with several people that he can get to his feet without spilling a drop. Soon everyone is around him, a thick circle of people cheering him on. Only Grace is left alone, sitting on the green leather chesterfield, waiting to be taken home.

BIRCHMOUNT LODGE HAS been built in a wooded area on the edge of town next to the new hospital. If your room faces west, you can sit by your window on a warm August evening like this and watch the sun disappear behind the trees into Georgian Bay. The afterglow in the sky is richly dramatic, even thrilling if such things are a cause for wonder and gratitude in your life. It doesn't seem at all a bad place to wait out the time remaining, but then I don't have to live here. Because the nursing home is some distance from my mother's house, I have driven over and now sit in my car in the parking lot. A few residents are taking the air near the entrance, some moving carefully along the pathways with the aid of metal walkers, others being pushed in wheelchairs by middle-aged daughters and sons. Louise Ouellette told me to be no later than eight o'clock, since her grandfather tires easily by the end of the day.

I have a moment or two, however, and so I remain in my car, weighed down by a sadness that may have something to do with all this evidence of mortal decline. Or perhaps it has to do with Pettinger and his twenty-year struggle that has ended with a bad book. The man and his manuscript have been on my mind all day. This sadness, however, may simply be caused by the time of year. When most people look for a pathetic fallacy to accompany their melancholic moments, they may choose a dismal evening of rain in November, or a January afternoon of wind and sleet. For me, though, sadness has often arrived at the end of a blazing August day when the warm light is bleeding into the darkness and I am alone.

As a child I had many such evenings when the town seemed abandoned and empty. This wasn't true, of course; you could hear children at their games on the next street: hide and go seek, red light, green light, run sheep run. But mother thought such children were too rough for me and so I was alone with her. Our supper of potato salad and cold ham and maple walnut ice cream was over and we had done the dishes together. Now my mother sat on the veranda reading a novel by A. J. Cronin or Lloyd C. Douglas. *The Keys of the Kingdom. The Robe. The Big Fisherman.* I remember such books in her hands and the reading glasses she had to wear by her mid-thirties. These gave her an even stricter and more demanding air. I would swing lazily in the hammock, thinking of the long evening ahead. The library books had gone stale, and all the best radio programs, "The Green Hornet," "The Great Gildersleeve," "Fibber McGee and Molly," were off the air for the summer. There seemed to be only piano music and plays about Greeks and Romans on the CBC. On such evenings I looked forward to the opening of school and the smell of new pencils and scribblers.

Sometimes my mother and I would go for a drive in the Dodge coupe, the dashboard lights glowing faintly as my mother shifted the stiff gears, and we moved carefully through the twilight at thirty miles an hour to Sandy Beach. There we could see the young people dancing in their bathing suits to the jukebox music at the Palace Pavilion and smell the fried onions and suntan oil. In the little snub-nosed Dodge coupe, mother and I seemed imprisoned, isolated from others whose lives included festivity and song. On such evenings I felt the absence of my father and saw clearly how it had diminished our world and reduced my mother and me to peculiar and pitiable spectators. If my mother felt anything like this, she never let on, nor would I have expected her to; for her, the drive to Sandy Beach was just an outing, "a breath of air," as she put it. On our way home, we stopped for ice-cream cones.

Winter evenings were far happier times for me, if only because I sensed that mother and I were then not so different from others. They too would be drying dishes or doing homework or listening to Mortimer Snerd on the radio as was I. It was in summer dusk that I imagined everyone else to be partaking in a feast to which I had not been invited. And it was on just such an August evening, following a day of recriminative rhetoric and catalogued shortcomings, that my wife left me, taking my son and daughter on a plane to Vancouver. After they left, I sat in the living room of our apartment and watched the shadows fill the room until night surrounded me. Late summer sadness.

In the foyer the old people are in wheelchairs by the front

door as though awaiting visitors. Or perhaps they just want to get out of their rooms for a while. The place is air-conditioned against the heat of the day, but the air seems dead, laden with the odours of sickness and old flesh. It can't be helped. The nursing home looks clean enough, but you can't escape the conditions: the sour gases of age, the decaying cells infecting the air. The woman at the front desk points down the hall and tells me that Mr. Fournier is in the last room on the right with two other gentlemen. Along the hallway residents push their aluminum walkers or hold on to the walls for support. If I last long enough, I too will become a part of this human wreckage one day.

In one corner of Leo Fournier's room there is a small colour television, and two old men are watching a comedy program. The laugh track spills over into the room. They hardly notice me as I pass. Leo Fournier is sitting in a chair by his bed looking out the window. Darkness is falling and I am struck by how short the days have become; in Ontario you begin to notice the approach of fall in the middle of August. Leo Fournier's name is on a little sign over his bed, but I can recognize the remnants of the young man in the back row of the team picture. He is now in his eighties and has sired eleven children. There are many grandchildren and great-grandchildren, an entire family carrying a part of him forward to other generations. And he still looks strong, a big man with powerful wrists and forearms. For years he worked at the shipyard. During the war, when they built Corvettes for the navy, Leo Fournier used a rivet gun. Louise told me all this. Now he sits in a blue tartan shirt and pants and bedroom slippers, a vigorous-looking old man with hair still dark and an angry hooded quality to his eyes. His skin is the colour of horse chestnuts and I suspect there is Indian blood in him. He is probably descended from the fur trappers and *coureurs de bois* who settled in this area two hundred years ago and married Indian women. His hands are folded in his lap.

"Mr. Fournier?" I begin. "My name is Howard Wheeler. I believe your granddaughter Louise told you I was coming to visit."

He turns his eyes upon me; they are clouded with cataracts. "Yes. Louise told me you would be coming."

He doesn't offer his hand and he seems distant, even reproachful. A man who greets strangers warily. A man who, when crossed in earlier times, would have quickly taken offence and settled matters with his fists. I have an image of him with his riveting gun on an August night in 1944, fastening steel plates to the sides of Corvettes that will plunge through the grey waves of the North Atlantic. As a child, during the war, I used to lie in bed listening through the screened windows to the sounds of the riveting guns as they were carried forth throughout the dark streets of the town. I show him the team photograph.

"Do you remember that picture, Mr. Fournier?"

He carefully takes the snapshot in his thick fingers as though afraid it might disintegrate or tear easily. The large heavy-knuckled hands show great respect for unfamiliar objects. He places the photograph in his lap and reaches into his shirt pocket for his reading glasses. Canned laughter from the TV bursts over the room. Once settled, the glasses give the old man a curious scholarly look. They are old-fashioned spectacles, round with black rims and they look incongruous on the big chestnut-coloured face. He inspects the photograph.

"Yes. That's the old team. That would be thirty-six or thirty-seven."

He turns over the picture as though searching for evidence of this.

"Thirty-five," I say. "The spring of nineteen thirty-five. You won the district championship and went on to the provincial intermediate semifinals and lost."

"Yes, I remember that," he says quietly. "It was a good series. We played Oshawa."

"What do you remember about my father, Mr. Fournier? Buddy Wheeler?"

Leo Fournier hands back the photograph. He is not a man affected by nostalgia, and I like that. He sees things straight on. No sentiment for bygone days. The best kind of witness to the past. Taking off his reading glasses, he returns them to his shirt pocket.

"Wheeler?" he says. "Right wing. A good hockey player. He could skate and stickhandle, that man. Very quick on his feet. I remember he had this cute little trick when he was going up the ice. He'd take a pass and push the puck onto his stick with his back skate. For a second or two he'd look like he was only skating on one leg. A helluva thing to see. But he was fast. They couldn't touch him out on open ice, so they always tried to get him in the corners and rough him up there. But he was usually too quick for them. Sometimes he would get hit and take a bad spill. He played with Crawford and Doucette and also with Thurso and Elmer Dumont. He scored a lot of goals for us. Buck Houle would play him on two lines because he was so good. He'd play thirty, forty minutes a game. Never seemed to get tired."

Leo Fournier's clouded eyes look past me.

"Then he didn't play with us for a couple of years. He went to Windsor or some place like that. He played a few games with Montreal one year, I think. That old Montreal team."

"The Maroons," I say.

"That's it. The Maroons. I think he was too small to stay in that league though there were some good small men in those days like Joliat and Boucher. I can't say for sure why he didn't stay with Montreal. He never talked about it when he came back to town."

The old man searches my face as though looking for signs of my father in me.

"He liked a drink too, your father," says Leo Fournier. "He liked a good time. We all did. I used to drink a fair amount. But then I stopped drinking twenty years ago. It was getting the better of me, eh! So I just stopped. I haven't had anything to drink in twenty years. Let me see that again."

He appears to have gained strength by this admission of his willpower, and Leo Fournier is not a man you easily refuse. I hand him back the picture, and he puts the glasses on again.

"That's Buck Houle the coach. Buck didn't know shit about coaching. He didn't show you anything. He just changed the lines."

He studies the picture, a serious old face behind spectacles.

"And Fowler," he says. "He called himself the manager, but he didn't manage anything. He was the owner. I wouldn't give that man the time of day. He was supposed to pay us ten dollars a game. All under the table, you understand. We were supposed to be amateurs. But you had to ask him for it, and then he would say he didn't have it. He always said he had no money. He would take his trouser pockets and turn them inside out and say, 'Look boys! They are just as empty as yours. These are hard times.' But we were filling the rink those years and he was paying his favourites. He brought in Hanna and Doucette. Got them jobs and paid them ten, fifteen dollars a game. That was damn good money in those days."

The old man now seems caught up in a long-buried grievance that I have innocently unearthed. He looks gloomily thoughtful as he returns the photograph. The glasses remain in place.

"Fowler paid his favourites. Doucette, Wheeler, Hanna, Thurso. He looked after them. The rest of us he forgot about."

He takes off his glasses and puts them in his shirt pocket. "We had some fun together though. There was always plenty to drink if you wanted it. There were lots of parties. Girls."

A mirthless smile crosses his face. "I could do this trick with a glass of beer. I used to do it at parties. Nobody else could do it but me. I used to make a few dollars betting with the boys."

"Is that so?"

"What I would do was lay down on my back on the floor and take a glass like this full of beer."

Leo Fournier takes a half-filled water glass from the windowsill and, after drinking the water, leans back in the chair staring at the ceiling. I can see the strong old cords in his neck and throat. He places the glass on his brow.

"I would," he says, "put the son of a whore right here on my forehead like this. Full of beer, mind you."

The glass is now resting on his forehead and slowly he takes his hands away and extends his arms until he looks like some strange crucified figure in a chair. One of the old roommates has turned from the television to watch him.

"I am on the floor with a glass of beer like this," Fournier continues, "and now I have to get up without spilling any."

Slowly he takes the glass away and straightening up looks at me in an unfriendly manner.

"You try that someday, mister."

"I couldn't do it. No point in trying."

He shrugs. "I suppose not. I could do it most of the time. If it was early and I wasn't too drunk."

"Did you like Buddy Wheeler?" I ask.

Again he shrugs. "Wheeler was all right. He was one of Fowler's favourite boys, but he was a damn good little hockey player. Nobody around here nearly as good. Bigger guys like me had to watch out for him because he was small, eh! He scored our goals for us, and so we had to watch out for him. I had nothing against the man."

Leo Fournier doesn't ask me what became of Buddy Wheeler: whether he survived and prospered, or sank beneath the burden of whatever troubles overwhelm some people. For Leo Fournier, my father ceased to exist the moment he left town; Buddy Wheeler will forever be a quick small man on skates who was one of George Fowler's favourites. Leo Fournier is not even interested in why I am sitting beside his bed on this summer night, staring at our reflections in the dark glass of the window. He is an enclosed old man of French-Canadian and Indian blood who once drank and played hockey with my father and worked at the shipyard and sired and raised eleven children. These are the facts of his life, and these are what he lives by. What else can you trust but the facts of your own life? Is there anything as reliable in theories or in books? Leo Fournier would probably say no. He would probably see little point in looking for truth in a book. Could such a man ever imagine another spending twenty years writing one?

When I leave, the long, lighted hallway is empty. The women in the white uniforms who look after the old people are settling them down for the night. As you pass the darkened doorways, you can hear their voices as they bend across beds. A great many pills are swallowed, I imagine, and fingers grasp the edge of sheets.

LINDA MACKLIN PHONED this morning. She wanted to know how I was getting on with Pettinger's manuscript. It seems the author has already called her office and made inquiries. He is probably beside himself these days, pacing around his farmhouse or tramping across the fields. His wife works in the garden and goes for a drive in the afternoons to get away from him. At two o'clock in the morning he wonders whether he has made the error of a lifetime, or is on the brink of redeeming himself and restoring the reputation of a forgotten literary man.

During our conversation Linda surprised me by saying that Pettinger had asked who was reading the manuscript, and when she told him, he seemed pleased. "A generational thing, I guess" was how Linda interpreted this. But I didn't think he would even remember me. He always did business with Del Shannon. I was just a dogsbody in the next office. I admitted to Linda that I found the novel heavy going in places and needed another week. I told her that I had to go into Toronto next Friday to see my doctor and I would let her know my opinion then. She seemed not to be listening.

"So how are you feeling anyway, Howard?"

"I'm all right."

"There is no hurry to rush back. We've got the spring list in place. It's very light. Everybody is cutting back. We may have to let a couple of people go."

Was she hinting at something, I wondered? Certainly they were getting along very nicely without me.

"This Pettinger thing," she said. "Unless we get some interest in New York, I don't really see how we can manage it."

I told her we shouldn't rush our decision. "It's a lifetime's work," I said. "The man is a serious writer."

Linda sounded either distracted or worried, perhaps both.

"Yeah well, whatever, Howard. Keep in touch. Okay? Ciao."

Linda's call unsettled me, and after climbing the stairs to my mother's bedroom where I had been reading, I stared at the cardboard boxes that held Pettinger's novel. I didn't really need another week; I didn't really need another minute. Yet I felt oddly protective about this huge, cranky misbegotten manuscript. It had taken Pettinger twenty years to write; the same amount of time it had taken my father to go from the quick small man on skates ("nobody around here could touch him") to the middle-aged drunk with a hole in his sock in the New American Hotel.

From the open window came that piercing sound that the cicada makes among the leaves of tall shade trees on summer days. As a youngster I had always thought it a peculiar song for an insect, and then years later someone told me that it wasn't a song at all. The creature produces the noise by rubbing its hind legs together. However he makes it, I always associate the sound with summer afternoons in this house.

Sitting in the rocking chair I read a few more pages of Pettinger's book, and then put aside the manuscript to look at a letter from my father to his young wife. There is something touching in old letters written by people who had little education. The writer was now forced to use language in an unfamiliar way. Words which could be used so prodigally in conversation had now to be weighed and measured and set down in a more orderly fashion. Words on paper suddenly assumed a permanence hitherto denied them. But this was a time before telephones were commonplace, and if you wanted to keep in touch with someone, you wrote a letter. Even people like my father, who never finished grade nine, could manage a reasonable degree of penmanship with a cheap fountain pen and a bottle of Waterman's ink. They got the blotters free from banks and insurance agents.

> 275 Cornelius Street
> Windsor, Ontario
>
> October 28, 1935
>
> Dear Gracie:
>
> Well, here I am in the big town of Windsor and ready to go. The train trip was fine and I was met

at the station by Mr. Carroll our coach and another player Reg Dick who is also trying to make the team. Reg is from up north somewheres near Sudbury. They put us up at Mrs. Wilson's place at the above address where you can write me. Mrs. Wilson seems like a nice lady. She sure has a lot of jokes and a big family. Mr. Wilson works for the CNR, I think he's a brakeman or something. There are about ten children so it's a little noisy in the house, but I am used to that having grown up with three sisters (ha ha!). Reg and me share a bedroom.

Mrs. Wilson is a good cook if tonight's supper was anything to go by. Pork chops and mashed potatoes and raisin pie. The family likes to kid each other a lot. I think they are going to be a swell bunch. Mrs. Wilson was surprised to find out I was married. Most of the players who have boarded here before have been single fellows. She wanted to know all about our baby. She loves babies. Her youngest is about two I guess and the others go all the way up to sixteen or seventeen. There are two sets of twins. But everyone seems to get along really good. We had our first practice today. It was fast and kind of rough, but I think I did okay. Coach Carroll seemed to be happy with how I played. I scored a goal in one of our scrimmages. Reg and me are going to the movies tonight with a couple of other guys from the team.

Take care of yourself.

Your loving husband,

Ross

P.S. Give the baby a kiss for me.
P.P.S. I am sorry again about last Saturday night.
You were right when you said I should know bet-
ter. I do know better, that's just it. I guess it's time
I started acting my age, Gracie.

During the summer of 1935 George Fowler pulled some
strings and got my father a try-out with the Windsor Bulldogs, a farm team of the Montreal Maroons who that
spring had won the Stanley Cup under T. P. Gorman. It
was unusual for an intermediate level player to go directly
into a professional league and the sports page of the
Huron Falls Times for October 23, 1935, noted as much.
Sports editor Chip McNeil headlined his story "Wheeler
Gets Pro Try-out at Windsor."

> This weekend local hockey star Buddy Wheeler
> leaves for Windsor, Ontario, and a try-out with the
> Bulldogs, the Stanley Cup Champion Maroons'
> top farm team in the International League. The
> blond-haired, smooth-skating right-winger who
> potted over forty goals with the Flyers last season
> is excited about the try-out, but not boastful. In an

interview this week, Buddy said, "I'll do my best. It won't be easy because there will be a lot of good veteran players on the team. But I am very grateful to Mr. Fowler and Mr. Gorman for giving me the chance." We wish Buddy all the best at Windsor, but making that team will be a real challenge for one of our town's finest young athletes.

Buddy was to leave for Windsor on the morning of Sunday, October 27. It had been arranged that George Fowler would drive him down to Union Station in Toronto where he would board the Windsor train. Grace packed Buddy's valise in the room in which I am now sitting, putting in sweaters and shirts and long underwear for the winter months ahead. She was now resigned to this change in their lives and in some ways was impressed by Buddy's new attitude and habits. This whole hockey business about which she had been so skeptical seemed to have matured him over the past several weeks. All summer he had been careful about his physical condition. He had not played softball for fear of injuring a hand or twisting an ankle. For Grace, the most agreeable consequence of that decision was that he did not accompany the softball players to Sandy Beach drinking parties after games. In fact, he drank no alcohol at all that summer. He told her he was serious about keeping in shape. Three mornings a week he went up to the high school on Falls Road and ran around the cinder track. In the afternoons, he worked out in the basement with a set of dumbbells borrowed from the YMCA.

By managing her household budget with special care, Grace was able to save here and there and she fed him beefsteak and ice cream. Over the summer he gained weight and muscle. In the evenings, they walked about the neighbourhood, wheeling their infant son in a large wicker carriage, a gift from Grandfather Stewart. It was unquestionably the happiest few weeks of their marriage.

On the Sunday morning in October that he is to leave, however, Grace is angry with him. She is in a bristling humour as she packs the clothes and toiletries into his new black travelling bag. The night before he fell off the wagon and Grace is furious with him, and his sisters. They just don't know any better, those people, is how Grace sees it. The sisters had organized a going-away party at the Wheelers' house on Dock Street. Martha and Muriel had come up from Toronto, and there were hockey players and their wives and girlfriends. A houseful of people and most of them were drunk by ten o'clock. Old Joe Wheeler got out his fiddle and scraped away at various jigs and reels. At one point things got entirely out of hand and there was a scuffle in the backyard. In the crisp October night two men in vests and shirtsleeves circled one another with their fists in the air. A dozen others looked on, and excited by the commotion, a neighbour's dog barked endlessly. It was a bear garden. A disgraceful exhibition. The last straw. And Grace, fuming, walked home alone. It was all so stupid. How could they expect him to succeed when they filled his body with that poison? Hours later Mildred brought her brother home and Grace got up to let them in;

together the two women helped Buddy up the stairs and into bed.

Aunt Mildred told me about that night when I visited her over forty years later in her little bungalow in what used to be called Leaside in east Toronto. At the time we were both grieving; she had just lost her husband to cancer, and I had lost my family. We were both in a sentimental mood and she had pictures to show me and stories to tell.

I liked Aunt Mildred. She had been dealt a rough hand in life but she was no complainer. The man she married, my Uncle Alf, looked like a good catch. He was handsome and funny and had a steady job with the Neilson company. Uncle Alf was an early hero of mine, a man who on summer visits handed out Jersey Milk chocolate bars. He and Aunt Mildred looked splendid in their Nash automobile. But he joined the army and it ruined him. Something happened during his years in the service; it was never clear just what, but drinking and perhaps theft of government property were hinted at in whispered conversations between my parents. After the war Uncle Alf seemed always to be ill and jobless, a thin man with a pencil moustache who no longer drank because of stomach ulcers. Even as a ten-year-old child, I could see in that narrow ruined face, with its wispy moustache, some terrible collapse of spirit and will. Later he had some kind of disability pension, but Aunt Mildred supported them for years by working as a waitress in the coffee shop of one of the big downtown hotels. They were childless, and when I spoke to Aunt Mildred in her living room in Leaside, she was the last of the Wheeler family, an aging widow and careworn by then though still pleasant looking. In her face you could see the good-natured waitress who traded jokes with businessmen as she served them their toasted westerns and coffee. She still remembered the night they had the party for Buddy, and her father playing the fiddle and the fistfight in the backyard.

"Boy, was your mother mad that night, Howard!" she said. "She left early and walked home by herself. Poor Bud. He hadn't been drinking for weeks. Hadn't touched a drop. And for that you can thank your mother. I'll be honest with you, Howard, we all thought your mother was a pretty straight-laced piece of goods in those days. Too strict about things. Do you know what I mean? But she was right about Bud. He was one of those men who can't handle their liquor. Alf was another. Your mother realized that but the rest of us couldn't see it at the time. And boy did she have him on the straight and narrow that summer! He was in training before he went down to Windsor, you see. And then Martha and Muriel and me, well, we thought it would be a good idea to give your father a little send-off with all his friends. And your dad was popular, Howard, he had a lot of friends in that town. But he just wasn't used to the liquor and he got pretty high that night. Martha's husband and me, we took him home. I had to get your mother out of bed, and the two of us got him up the stairs. You could almost see the smoke coming out of your mother's ears. She kept saying, 'He should know better. You should all know better.' She wouldn't talk to me or any of us for weeks after. She was that mad."

So, on the morning of the departure, Buddy is contrite and pale, a little sick in body and heart, stepping carefully around his wife while she packs his bag. In a few minutes Fowler will be picking him up and taking him away from her. She resents Fowler's influence. She knows that it is really Fowler and not she who has wrought this change in her husband. When Buddy comes into the bedroom he is dressed in the suit he was married in; it's now a little tight but he still looks presentable. The alarm clock on the dresser says ten minutes to eight. Buddy is going to try to put the best face on things. After all, he is going away; it would be a shame to leave with sour feelings between them.

"Well, Gracie," he says, "what do you think? Do I look okay? Do you think I'll pass muster in Windsor?"

She ignores him. Her back is to him as she closes the clasps of his bag. She still cannot meet his eyes. Restoring cordiality after these tiffs has always been a problem for her.

"You look fine, Ross," she says quietly.

He must make the first move. This he has learned after fourteen months of life under the same roof. Standing behind her he places his hands on her elbows and kisses the back of her neck.

"I'm sorry about last night, Gracie."

"You should know better, Ross."

"I know that. Sorry."

She goes to the closet and returns with a large brown paper package. "I bought something for you," she says handing him the package. "A going-away present."

She still looks cross, but the air has cleared, a signal for him to give way to high spirits and tomfoolery.

"A present? For me? Ah, Gracie!"

He likes to make a fuss over gifts and small surprises and she is not displeased by these performances. They already form a little ritual in their life together.

"What can it be? Oh, what can it be?" he says as he tears away the brown paper to disclose a Biltmore hat box. Was it, I wonder, the same box I saw in his closet at the New American Hotel? Inside the box is a new grey fedora with a burgundy band. Buddy is delighted.

"Why, Gracie, this is really something!"

Standing before the dresser mirror, he carefully places the hat upon his head, dipping at the knees to get a better view of himself. He looks extraordinarily happy.

"I would say very smart, Gracie, wouldn't you? Oh very, very smart."

Turning, he clasps her about the waist and lifts her off her feet. "You are my one and only girl."

Frowning she protests, "Let me down, Ross. There's something else."

He lets go of her and she hands him a book.

"Here is something for winter nights," she says.

He stares at *A Treasury of Good Stories* and nods, smiling. In it are tales by Conan Doyle and W. W. Jacobs, Edgar Allan Poe and Saki. A dozen other masters of old. He will start such stories many times over the next few months but seldom finish them. *A Treasury of Good Stories* will go largely unread though he will carry it from hotel to hotel throughout his travels. The book is inscribed: "To my husband. With good wishes for future success. Grace. October 1935." This touches him.

"This is really swell of you, Gracie."

From the street below comes the sound of an automobile horn.

"That's Mr. Fowler now," says Buddy, going to the window and parting the curtains. "He's got the new LaSalle too. He told me he was going to let me drive."

Grace is frowning again. Why can't the man show some courtesy and come to the door instead of sitting in his car blowing the horn? Summoning her husband to him like a servant! But she now expects no less from George Fowler. Without having openly declared war, they are enemies. In the past year, each has crossed King Street at least once to avoid speaking. By sitting in his new car, Fowler wants her to know that he is running things in Buddy's life.

Downstairs, Buddy, more excited than she can ever remember seeing him, kisses his child and wife. Then, in his overcoat and new fedora and carrying his valise, he runs down the veranda steps to the big grey car. Grace stands watching by the open door, smelling the sharp clear morning. There is hoarfrost on the grass. George Fowler has climbed out of the car and opened the trunk. A gentleman, thinks Grace, would at least have touched the brim of his hat in acknowledgement of her presence in the front doorway. But Fowler is such a spiteful boor. She finds it actually invigorating to hate such a man. To wish him ill and hope to see him brought low unto the stables of humility. Fowler hands Buddy the keys and Grace watches her husband wave a final time. Then both men get in the car. Behind the curtains of the parlour window, our house-keeper Violet Day holds me in her arms, swaying gently to keep me quiet.

When my mother returned to Dufferin Street Public School in September of that year, she hired Violet Day to look after me and help run the house. Women nowadays think nothing of returning to work a few months after having a baby, but in 1935 it was uncommon; moreover, such a woman was regarded by most other women as neglectful. A mother's place was in the home and Grace Wheeler was the subject of many conversations over back fences and kitchen tables.

Violet Day was then in her late thirties, I suppose. She lived with her elderly mother a few blocks away and was considered "odd," as people used to say. This was doubt-less because of the enormous raspberry-coloured birth-mark that disfigured one side of her face and condemned her to estrangement. A lifetime with this terrible rebuke from nature had left her intensely withdrawn, a deeply troubled woman, though kindness itself in looking after me. That huge flaming blemish was an early and impor-tant image in my life. I awoke to it in my crib and stared at it while Violet changed my diapers or fed me. Many times I must have reached up to touch it before falling asleep while she rocked me by the kitchen window, listen-ing to "Ma Perkins," or "Pepper Young's Family." I remember Violet's long apron and her lisle stockings and her plain brown shoes with straps across the insteps. They reminded me of the sandals worn by the apostles in a book of illustrated Bible stories I was given one Christmas.

As she moved further into middle age, Violet withdrew more and more into a part of herself that was private and secret. In the end she became an unmanageable burden to her mother. Some years later she struck the old woman one last time, and was confined to the asylum in Penetanguishene where my mother visited her once a month until Violet's death in the early 1950s. But on that Sunday in late October 1935, Violet Day was downstairs in the kitchen of this house, peeling potatoes and carrots and turnips for dinner which was eaten at one o'clock. Grace would have been in this room dressing for church and waiting for her father who now picks her up each Sunday. Time heals wounds and after the service they return to this house to eat dinner together. The old man enjoys looking at his grandson, a happy surprise for Grace.

While she is dressing for church, Buddy and George Fowler are southbound on Highway 11, a narrow ribbon of pavement that traverses a countryside of ploughed fields and stubble, passes through towns and villages with English names like Barrie, Bradford, Churchill, Newmarket, Richmond Hill, and becomes finally Yonge Street, Toronto's main thoroughfare. The smoke from Fowler's cigar makes Buddy light-headed, but he is careful not to say anything. Because of Mr. Fowler, he is being given the chance to play professional hockey, a childhood dream. You don't tell a man who has made such things come to pass to put out his cigar. Especially if you are driving his new LaSalle sedan.

The two men talk mostly about motor cars and hockey. Will the Maroons win the Stanley Cup again? Fowler likes their chances, but Buddy thinks Toronto and Detroit have good teams and will be tough. And don't lose sight of Chicago either! The big car surges forth under the pressure of Buddy's foot on the gas pedal. Fowler glances at the speedometer.

"Not too fast, Bud. She's just broken in. She handles nicely though, doesn't she?"

"It's a swell car, Mr. Fowler."

"You'll like Dick Carroll and Harris Ardiel," Fowler says. "They're good men. They'll give you a fair shake. All you have to do is work hard and do your best. Watch the booze! A beer here and there and no harm done. That's not what I'm talking about. Know what I mean?"

Buddy nods.

"It's easy," says George Fowler, "for a young fellow to pick up bad habits in this business, so don't embarrass me, Bud. I'm going out on a limb here. I've talked to Tommy Gorman about you, so I don't want to be embarrassed. Work hard. That's all I ask."

"I will, Mr. Fowler. You can depend on me."

"I hope so," says Fowler, looking out the window at the stark blue sky. "And watch the girls! You're a married man now, Bud, remember that," he adds with what seems to be a chuckle.

Is it Buddy's imagination or does he detect the possibility

that Fowler is making fun of his marriage? It's sometimes hard to tell with the man. Buddy glances sideways at Fowler's large fleshy cheeks and then turns his attention back to the road, wondering.

In Union Station, cavernous and grey and echoing with loudspeaker sounds, Fowler buys him coffee and apple pie and cheese. They sit in a booth listening to the booming announcements of arriving and departing trains. Around them the station is filled with hurrying, distracted travellers. Now and then, when he really thinks of what is happening in his life, Buddy feels a lurch in his stomach. His new valise with his skates in the bottom is secured between his knees. He is anxious now to be on his way; he and Fowler are talked out. A final handshake and Buddy walks away to stand in line for the train to Windsor.

Once aboard he takes a seat by the window. As the train gathers speed, Buddy looks out at freight yards and factories and the back lots of houses. He feels queasy with nerves and hangover sickness, and after a few minutes he makes his way to the toilet. There, with his hand on the flushing lever, he bends over to vomit forth coffee and apple pie and cheese. Afterwards he washes his face and combs his hair and takes a peppermint for his breath.

I HAD THOUGHT TO WORK on Pettinger's manuscript this morning, and for an hour or so, despite the vacuum cleaner sounds from downstairs, I managed. The current chapter is a savage excursion into why and how the internal combustion engine will finish us off sooner or later. Pettinger's hero has now reached the year 1923 and he is working for a vicious capitalist, a Henry Ford type, who is turning out each day thousands of "mechanically sound black automobiles." There is a euphoric mood throughout North America and men with vision foresee our continent criss-crossed with highways. And on these highways will be millions of these black automobiles. Factory smoke is soiling the skies. Ahead lie the Depression, the Hitler war, the arms build-up and the growth of Texas, the Beatles, Vietnam, Asian economic hegemony, environmental collapse, the whole mad enterprise according to Pettinger. And for all I know, he may be right. In any case, I had to stop at 1923 because Mrs. Chernyk phoned.

A couple wanted to see the house and they were pressed for time. Could they come around right away? Mrs. Chernyk sounded hopeful. "Two schoolteachers from Toronto," she said. "They have both accepted jobs up here and they want to get settled before the school year begins. The man is going to teach the making and fixing of things at the high school. What do you call it?"

"I'm not sure nowadays, Mrs. Chernyk," I said. "Industrial arts maybe?"

"That's it," she said. "Industrial arts. He is going to teach that at the high school. His wife has a job too. At one of the elementary schools. But here is the thing, Mr. Wheeler. The man is what you would call handy. He can build and fix things. And they want an older house on a quiet street with big trees. I told him that your mother's house is just what they are looking for, but it only has one bathroom. And do you know what he said, Mr. Wheeler?"

"Probably what ten million other people in this country say every day, Mrs. Chernyk, 'No problem.'"

Mrs. Chernyk was silent. For a moment I thought she'd hung up on me. Finally she said, "You must be a reader of minds, Mr. Wheeler. That's exactly what he said. 'No problem.' How did you know that?"

"Just a guess, Mrs. Chernyk."

"Well, if it's all right, I'd like to bring them around right away. I think I am going to sell your mother's house today, Mr. Wheeler."

I explained about Louise Ouellette and the vacuum cleaner, but that presented no difficulty for Mrs. Chernyk, and so I hung up feeling oddly ambivalent about her call. Now that the house might actually be sold, I was uneasy.

Another family would take possession of what had always been my home. At the same time, wasn't that what the whole exercise was about? Getting rid of the place and getting back to Toronto and the rest of my life?

Downstairs Louise was poking the snout of the vacuum cleaner underneath the sofa in the parlour. When I interrupted her to say that we would soon be having visitors, she merely nodded and continued with her work. Earlier Louise had asked me about my visit to her grandfather. I told her that our talk had been useful, and this seemed to surprise her.

"He doesn't say much, does he?" she said. "We go up to see him on Sundays, and he sits there and we look at him and he looks at us."

She was filling a pail with water at the kitchen sink, a cigarette in her mouth. With a bandanna around her hair, she looked like a wartime factory hand. Rosie the Riveter!

"Did he remember your father?" she asked.

"Oh, yes," I said. "Your grandfather remembered him. But I got the impression that he didn't like him very much."

"Is that so?" said Louise. "Well, I better get started."

She ran cold water over the cigarette and threw the butt into the wastebasket. That was it. She was not going to pursue the matter any further. Like her grandfather, Louise is not greatly interested in the details of other people's lives.

On the veranda I wait for Mrs. Chernyk and the schoolteachers. They arrive within ten minutes. In her yellow blazer and black slacks Mrs. Chernyk looks brisk and businesslike as she escorts the couple up the front walk.

The wife is small and perky, eager to please, one of those women who are often described as dynamic. I can see her sitting on the floor with her grade two class reading a story. She would get on my nerves in no time. The husband has a different metabolism: older, slower, a rather grave, patient-looking fellow. And would these two now share my mother's house? I leave them to Mrs. Chernyk and take a walk for my health.

On this brilliant August morning I can smell petunias and their fragrance is as resonant for me as Proust's madeleines were for him. This smell of petunias brings to mind a childhood impatience to begin again with new lined scribblers and freshly sharpened Ticonderoga pencils and oak and maple leaves pressed between the pages of books. My walk this morning takes me away from these leafy streets, Queen, Dufferin, Princess, with their large brick houses, to Dock Street. Here my grandparents raised three girls and a boy in an unpainted frame house with an outdoor toilet and a chicken coop in the backyard. Beyond lay the train tracks and coal yards and Georgian Bay.

Dock Street is now more respectable with its aluminum-sided bungalows and carports. Most of these houses were built at the end of the war for returning soldiers. Wartime houses they were called in those days, small frame dwellings, cheap and utilitarian. When they were built, both my grandparents were dead and my aunts were all married and living in Toronto. As I walk, I picture Dock Street as it was when the Wheeler family lived here; when my father was growing up and playing with his sisters and other children. In those days it was poor in a way that would be unimaginable in an Ontario town any more. People then lived in houses that today would be condemned by the authorities: ramshackle places with tar-paper sides. Many had no indoor plumbing and some had no electricity. I can remember coal-oil lamps in windows along this street and that was during the war.

In those days, the poor were more easily recognizable, especially the children, who often had ringworm and head lice. There were more crossed eyes then and crooked teeth. In the summer children's faces broke open with impetigo and their eyes were puffy with sties. In the winter you could smell their underwear and feet when they came in from the cold and stood by the classroom radiators. When they got sick, the doctor nailed quarantine signs to the front doors of their houses warning visitors to stay away from scarlet fever or diphtheria.

The street, of course, was unpaved in those times, nothing more than a dirt road. There were woodpiles by the sides of houses. Here and there an old tire hung from a tree branch, a child's homely swing. The sheets on the clotheslines behind the houses were speckled with soot from the passing trains. On summer evenings women sat on their front stoops to get a little air and men tinkered with old cars that never ran. On moonless nights in the fall, men and older boys took burlap bags and crossed the railway tracks to the coal yards.

All this has now changed except for the railway tracks. They are still here, looking much the same as they did fifty or a hundred years ago. Railway tracks remind us of an age that had not yet discovered lighter materials like aluminum and plastic. They make me think of my grandfather Stewart in the foundry among such heavy objects of everyday use as cast-iron stove lids and pokers. Or the old prewar automobiles my father sold at Fowler Motors. Stand in front of a meat and potatoes car from the thirties, say a 1937 Pontiac. Mark its heft and weight: headlamps, grillwork, fenders, bumper; here you are looking at the labour of men who worked in a world of materials far heavier than ours.

These railway tracks remind me too of how much time my father must have spent on trains the year he played hockey for Windsor in the International League. That year he travelled to cities like Buffalo and Syracuse, Cleveland and Pittsburgh, the very epicentre of the old steel age. Looking out coach windows at afternoons of grey rain or fields stiff with snow in winter sunlight. Around him the shenanigans of young men travelling together: card games, bawdy stories, practical jokes, cigar smoke, beer farts. He did well that year. He was twenty-three and this was his burnished moment. With his letters he sent my mother clippings from the *Windsor Star*. These he probably cut from the paper while sitting in his long underwear on the edge of his bed at Mrs. Wilson's.

ROOKIE SCORES TWO AS BULLDOGS EDGE ROCHESTER

Rookie Buddy Wheeler led the Bulldogs to victory over the Rochester Cardinals last night at the

Arena, scoring twice as the locals defeated the visitors 3-2. Wheeler notched the winner with just eight minutes left in the game when he took a pass from Dave Downie and rifled a hard, rising shot from just inside the blue line. The Rochester goalkeeper was completely fooled by the youngster's hard drive.

Some of his letters were written on the train. If you bought the right kind of ticket, you could deal with your correspondence in the club car. You could sit at a desk complete with blotter and inkwell. To secure your stationery against the swaying motion, you attached it to the blotter by means of a little clip. At such desks salesmen calculated their day's business, and maiden aunts wrote to favourite nephews, enclosing two-dollar bills and fondest regards to your mother and father. But a hockey player travelling from Windsor to Pittsburgh wrote his letters in the coach, knees up with stocking feet on the opposite seat, a book (*A Treasury of Good Stories*?) anchoring his page. Sometimes the swirls and loops in my father's handwriting suggest a lurch in the train's motion: the writer's pen miscarries on *a*, *t* or an *l* as the coach leans into a curve; the writer pauses before the next sequence of words, his attention arrested by the front of the train rounding the curve, the line of coaches, the baggage cars, the smoking locomotive pulling that immense weight across the surface of the earth at eighty miles an hour.

When I return to the house, Louise is finishing up and the place smells of floor wax and lemon oil. There is a message for me to phone Mrs. Chernyk, but I am not up to it at the moment. The walk has tired me. After a cup of tea and a tomato sandwich, I climb the stairs to my mother's bedroom. The shadows of leaves on the walls and the distant drone of a lawn mower are soothing to me. In the quiet ticking of the house I read one of my father's letters. It was written hurriedly on the train to Montreal late in the winter of 1936. Good fortune had entered his life and he was eager to share these tidings with my mother.

Friday, March 6, 1936

Dear Gracie:

Something really great has happened. I told you how I am having a pretty good year at Windsor. Well I got another goal against Syracuse the other night and Coach Carroll came to me and said that he was talking on the phone to Mr. Gorman, and he would like me to come up for a few games with the Maroons. They are in a real battle with the Leafs for first place, and it seems they have injuries with Robinson and Lamb both hurt. They need a right-winger and Coach Carroll told Mr. Gorman that I have been playing really good hockey since Christmas. Anyway Mr. Gorman wants to have a look at me. I phoned Mr. Fowler and asked him if he would let you know about this and he said he would. But I wanted to write you anyway. Keep your fingers crossed for me, Gracie. Somehow I will try to mail this when I get to Montreal.

Your loving husband,

Ross

P.S. The Detroit Red Wings, the team the Maroons are going to play tomorrow night, are on this same train. What do you think of that? They were all eating in the dining car today and I recognized some of them from pictures in the paper. I saw Larry Aurie and Herbie Lewis and Goodfellow. It's hard to believe I might be playing against these guys tomorrow night.

P.P.S. Give my love to the baby.

What do you think of that? he asks her. Not much, I suspect. Mother was not easily impressed by those who make their way in this world with a hockey stick or a ball and bat. The names of those hockey players who were stars in their day would have meant nothing to her. This whole episode was probably seen as a distraction from the real business of living. As far as she was concerned, her husband was now twenty-three years old and still playing a game, for goodness sakes. She was incapable of appreciating the sense of wonder and anticipation so evident in his words. Presbyterians are suspicious of enthusiasm, for who knows where it may lead? Warnings are routinely issued against the likelihood of vainglory: "Remember that pride goeth before a fall;" "Just don't get too big for your britches, Mister." Ontario towns are filled with older people who, like myself, grew up with such admonitions in our ears. They are as familiar to us as are mantras to a Hindu.

Nor could my mother share in her imagination Buddy Wheeler's eager, nervous afternoon on that train to Montreal as he sat in the dining car in his ill-fitting suit, staring at his cheese omelette and listening to the Detroit players talking and laughing. Looking out at old snow along cedar rail fences and the grey water of Lake Ontario in March. And the towns along its northern shore: Port Hope, Cobourg, Belleville, Kingston, Brockville, Cornwall. His stomach, which would give him trouble in the years ahead, must have been in knots. Would someone steal his skates while he was eating?

He phoned his news to George Fowler because we had no telephone at the time. My frugal mother saw no need to pay a company each month for a device that she could foresee lying silent and useless most of the day and night. What was the point? It was a rebuke to thrift. Any emergency could be dealt with by crossing the street to a neighbour who had a telephone. It didn't seem to occur to my mother that such visits could be viewed as a nuisance by the neighbour. How could they be when they so rarely occurred? If you lived sensibly, most emergencies could be avoided. Such implacable logic was difficult to combat. When, a year later, my grandfather Stewart had to be taken to the hospital in the final stages of his cancer, it was that neighbour who came to our house with the news. Shortly thereafter mother had a telephone installed.

In March 1936, however, she received my father's good news in a roundabout way. According to the envelope postmark, the letter wasn't mailed until the following Monday, March 9. All that weekend my father carried it around in his pocket, probably too excited and distracted to think clearly. He may even have thought of throwing it away; after all, it was old news by then. Nevertheless, he slipped it into a letter box, perhaps on his way to a Monday morning practice in company with an older player who stopped on the slushy Montreal street to wait for him: "Come along, young fellow, or we'll be late and Tommy will skin our hides."

How then did she discover that he was on his way to Montreal and a chance with the Stanley Cup champion Maroons? Aunt Mildred told me part of the story on that afternoon years later in her living room in Leaside. George Fowler ignored my father's request and did not tell my mother. That would have involved going around to her house and knocking on the door and standing there waiting to be admitted. He was damned if he'd knock on that woman's door like a delivery boy. Buddy was a good kid right enough, but his wife was a pain in the keester. Now Buddy's sister Mildred was a different kettle of fish. There was a woman you could chew the fat with and have a few laughs. Didn't think herself so high and mighty as the uppity schoolteacher. Mildred Wheeler was the real goods. And dance? It was something to see her and Buddy dancing at the Christmas party. No two ways about it, Mildred was a damn good sport.

At this time Mildred was the only one still living at home with the "old people," as my Wheeler grandparents were always called by their children. Mildred was a pretty young woman with short blond hair and a good figure. She worked as a cashier at Woolworth's for twelve dollars a week. People around town liked her; she was popular but not fast. There was no shortage of young men to take her dancing at the Blue Room on Saturday nights, but she was not sweet on anyone in particular, and it was understood that you could only go so far with her in the back seat after the dance. She enjoyed a drink or two but knew her limits. Like her brother, she adored the movies and went to the Capitol Theatre as often as her pocket-book allowed. Six days a week she stood behind the cash machine and rang up sales for ten-cent combs or two for a quarter dish towels or thirty-five-cent framed photos of Jean Harlow or Clark Gable.

And it is here in Woolworth's on King Street that George Fowler begins the business of relaying the news of Buddy Wheeler's ascension to the National Hockey League. Woolworth's is a store that a man like George Fowler seldom frequents, and so his presence on Friday morning causes clerks and a few housewives fingering tablecloths to cast shy glances his way. Mildred is pleasantly surprised to see him.

"Why, Mr. Fowler," she smiles. "How are you this morning?"

Fowler touches the brim of his grey hat with thumb and forefinger and offers Mildred a foxy grin.

"How are tricks, Mildred?"

She laughs. To her, Fowler is a harmless old flirt and she can play him like a banjo.

"Tricky, Mr. Fowler. Tricky."

On this morning Mildred is wearing a navy blue dress with a choker of cultured pearls, a Christmas gift from Buddy. It is her best outfit, and she likes to wear it on Fridays because that is their busiest day. Stout and grinning, George Fowler leans in on the counter. She can smell the bay rum on his jowls.

"Mildred," he says, lowering his voice like a man about to traffic in confidences, "I don't know if you've heard this one, but there was this Irishman, this Englishman and this Jew . . ."

Fowler knows how to tell a story; over a lifetime he has related thousands of them in club cars and hotel lobbies and dressing rooms. When he finishes his tale of the three mythical figures, he is delighted by Mildred's laughter. My aunts had a risible side to them, and as a young child at family gatherings, I always marvelled at the ease with which they would explode into laughter over a story. To my mother, of course, Mildred and her sisters were all "laughers" who couldn't be taken seriously.

And so with the comical anecdote out of the way, George Fowler removes his gloves and unbuttons his heavy coat against the dry heat of the store.

"Buddy telephoned last night," he says.

A look of mild worry crosses Mildred's face. Without question her brother is the most important person in her life at the moment.

"How is he, Mr. Fowler? Is he okay?"

"Our boy is grand, Mildred. He couldn't be better." Fowler pauses for dramatic emphasis. "He's been called up by the Maroons."

Mildred follows hockey. She goes to the Flyers' games at the Arena Gardens and she now keeps track of the scores and standings in the International League. If she doesn't have a date on a Saturday evening, she will listen to Foster Hewitt describe the game from Maple Leaf Gardens while she irons or reads a movie magazine. She even has a favourite player in the NHL: Toronto right-winger Charlie Conacher, one of Lionel's younger brothers and a member of the famous Kid Line. So Fowler's news has a significance for her that it wouldn't have for my mother.

"No kidding?" Mildred says. "Will he be on the radio, do you think?"

"Not any station that we can listen to, Mildred," says Fowler. "They play in Montreal tomorrow night against the Red Wings. However, they'll be in Toronto a week from Saturday. If he's still with the team." Fowler shrugs as though to suggest that stranger things have happened in this old world of ours.

Mildred can't wait to pass on this news to anyone who will listen.

"Gee, that's really swell, Mr. Fowler."

"Yes. This is an excellent opportunity for him, Mildred. And it's good news for the town too. Local boy in the big league. It can't hurt a bit."

He begins to adjust his scarf and rebutton his heavy coat. As he draws on his gloves, he smiles at her.

"Mildred? Do you think you could do me a big favour?"

"Why sure, Mr. Fowler."

Fowler lays his gloved hands on the counter.

"I've got a dozen things to do this morning. Could you pass the good news on to Buddy's better half?"

If Mildred detects any meanness in the clumsy irony of Fowler's term, she doesn't let on. But probably she misses what is there. Like her brother, Mildred approaches human affairs in a spirit of ingenuousness. Why would people bother to be nasty to one another? What is to be gained by such behaviour? To Mildred, the kind of psychological warfare waged by people like my mother and George Fowler would be incomprehensible.

"Sure, Mr. Fowler," she says. "I'll be glad to."

"You're a good girl, Mildred," says Fowler waving. "Don't take any wooden nickels now."

"You can bet I won't," she laughs.

It doesn't appear to bother Fowler that he is putting Mildred Wheeler to considerable inconvenience. After being on her feet all day working the cash register, she must now walk across town to Queen Street which is in the opposite direction to her own home. But Mildred doesn't really mind. She will be glad to tell Grace the news, and while doing so she will get to hold her nephew. Mildred loves babies and it will be one of the cruel ironies of her life that she and Alf will be unable to have children. At Grace's house she will have to suffer her sister-in-law's remote and condescending manner. Muriel is intimidated by it and Martha laughs it to scorn, but Mildred accepts the idea that some people are like that. They can't help being what God made them, and you shouldn't take their standoffishness or whatever you want to call it personally.

As I discovered, however, my mother already knew about my father's move by the time Aunt Mildred had arrived at our front door. Years later I asked her, "How did you find out that Dad was going to Montreal? Did he phone you?"

"We had no telephone at the time," she said.

"How then?" I asked.

"One of my pupils told me," she said and left it at that.

But I wanted details. Some flesh on the bones of this story. "What were the circumstances?" I persisted.

"Oh, I don't remember, Howard," she said looking mildly impatient. How could such a thing be of the slightest importance? "It was a long time ago," she added.

A long time ago, yes! But what happened? One of her pupils told her? How did he find out? I say *he* because I imagine it was a boy who told her. I also imagine that Aunt Mildred told every customer who stood before her that day. And by noon more than one of those customers had mentioned over lunch that Buddy Wheeler was now playing in the National Hockey League with the Montreal Maroons. It is not difficult to see a ten-year-old boy running like the

Athenian messenger with the news to the school yard on Dufferin Street.

At ten minutes to one Miss Hepworth comes out on the cement steps to ring the handbell that summons the children to classes. They form into two lines, boys on one side of the building and girls on the other! And please keep in line and no talking! As the grade five class files into Mrs. Wheeler's room to take their seats, one boy slowly makes his way to the front where Grace is writing on the blackboard the names of the province's counties: Huron, Haldimand, Lanark, Perth. A geography lesson will follow.

The boy assigned the task of verifying the wonderful news has been carefully chosen by his classmates. It is important that he get a respectful hearing, and so he can be neither sluggard nor ruffian. The chosen one is Lloyd Cardwell, a stolid youngster who pays attention in class and gets decent grades, but who can also handle tough customers at recess if they try any funny business. Mrs. Wheeler, they all agree, will listen to Lloyd. When he stands behind her, Grace stops writing to turn and look at him. What have we here? Lloyd Cardwell is a good boy, so what can it be? Surely not the toilet? He's had plenty of time for that. Grace frowns.

"Yes, Lloyd? What is it?"

In his slow, deliberate manner, Lloyd Cardwell delivers his carefully rehearsed question: "Is it true, Mrs. Wheeler, that Mr. Wheeler is now playing for the Maroons?"

My mother was never easily surprised. You couldn't startle her into open-mouthed wonder by anything under the sun. It was as though she half-expected that any day could reveal the full measure of life's obvious absurdities and reversals. I hear her responding to the boy's question with one of her own.

"And where did you hear that, Lloyd?"

"Russell Coombs told me," says Lloyd Cardwell. "He said his mother told him at lunch. She heard it downtown in one of the stores. She said that Mr. Wheeler has been called up by the Maroons and is going to play against Detroit tomorrow night."

How did she deal with this information? Probably in the only way she knew how. Even at the risk of appearing not to know what is going on in her family's life, she tells Lloyd Cardwell the truth.

"I've not heard that, Lloyd. It might very well be. Now please take your seat. I want to begin."

"Yes, Mrs. Wheeler."

And Lloyd Cardwell returns to his seat, now convinced that the story is untrue and Russell Coombs is a liar and he has been tricked. George Fowler's shabby behaviour has consequences far beyond his imagining.

Later in the afternoon, of course, Grace discovers that the story is true, confirmed by Mildred who stands in the front hall in her winter coat and hat ("I can only stay a minute, Grace"), holding the baby.

"Oh, what a darling you are! Yes, you are. Oh, Grace, he is so sweet!"

Of the three Wheeler sisters, Mildred is at least tolerable, in Grace's opinion. Watching her fuss over the baby,

Grace allows that her sister-in-law would probably make a good mother. But she should find a husband soon to take care of her before that figure slackens and her looks fade. All three sisters, Grace believes, will end up looking shapeless and grey like the mother.

THE HOUSE HAS BEEN SOLD. I have accepted the school-teachers' offer, and this afternoon I signed various papers in Mrs. Chernyk's office next to Valu-Mart at the corner of King and Wellington streets. On this site once stood the old Huron House where my mother watched her husband and sister-in-law foxtrot to the "Isle of Capri"; where Leo Fournier lay on the floor with a glass of beer on his forehead and rose heroically to his feet without spilling a drop.

By the window in Mrs. Chernyk's office, I looked out at a relentlessly sodden day. King Street was virtually deserted with only a few cars passing by, their tires hissing on the wet pavement. We were under one of those drenching late-summer rains that so often follow a dry spell. I remember welcoming such weather as a child. A day like this was for reading or poking around the house; it was somehow a comfort to know that everyone else was indoors like me. When this low pressure system passes through the region, the wind will veer into the northwest and push down cool, dry air. And summer will be over for another year.

Mrs. Chernyk seemed mildly put out by my subdued manner. I think she wanted praise for her efforts on my behalf, and so I hastened to oblige. I told her that she had done an excellent job.

"Well, older homes are not so easy to sell these days," she said. "Younger people want newer houses. As you may have observed, the couple was older. In the real estate business, Mr. Wheeler, we have a saying: when the right buyer meets the right house, we have a sale. A question of timing."

"Makes sense. Still, I think you did a fine job."

"It is kind of you to say so, but you don't seem as pleased as I would have expected. At the beginning of the summer, you were most anxious to get the house off your hands. I even detected some urgency in the matter."

All this was true, and, of course, a part of me was glad that it was over. What would I do with the place anyway? Yet selling the house you grew up in can wrench the heart; in a sense, you are abandoning a part of yourself forever. And no one is happy with *forever*.

Still it was done and I had to be clear of it all by the end of September. The lawyers would take over now. Mrs. Chernyk and I shook hands, and I made my way along the wet street to the public library. Weeks ago I had asked the estimable Mrs. Loomis if she could get for me the microfilm of the Montreal *Gazette* for March 1936. This morning she phoned to say that it had arrived, and indeed it is on the machine and waiting for me as I shake the rain from my Burberry and umbrella. At once I feel as snug as a bug in the bowels of the old stone building. Beyond the basement window water gushes from a drainpipe onto the grass while I turn the little wheel and watch the so-called news of another time pass before my eyes.

Here are dispatches from Abyssinia where troops of the grotesque Mussolini are marching against black men armed with spears. Here are pictures of absurd old fogies in frock coats and starched collars: Stanley Baldwin, Baron von Neurath, W. L. Mackenzie King. There are buffoons in dress uniform like Generalissimo Franco and A. Hitler. Here is the photograph of a child, a six-year-old girl with a bandaged head; one eye has been torn loose from its socket by a wayward dog. And here is an account of a gangster, mowed down by the cops in an alleyway in St. Louis, Missouri. And a story of young lovers fleeing angry parents, locked in a "death embrace" in her father's sedan. The same old terrible stories, and all the characters have now vanished along with the men and women who recorded their dismal adventures.

On the sports pages for Monday, March 9, is an account of Saturday night's game in which the Montreal Maroons had a fairly easy time defeating the Detroit Red Wings 5-3. My father draws a sentence near the end. "With the injury to Earl Robinson, the Maroons called up Buddy Wheeler from Windsor, but the young right-winger saw little action in Saturday's contest." Two nights later, the Maroons and the New York Rangers play a scoreless tie. According to the reporter, the highlight of this game appears to have been a fight between New York's Art Coulter and the Maroons' Lionel Conacher. Reading about this has a poignancy all its own, for I remember that folded newspaper clipping beneath my father's shirts and socks in the New American Hotel. Lionel Conacher's obituary!

Buddy Wheeler, then, fails to impress the *Gazette*'s reporter or probably anyone else in his first two big league games. He went for a skate, as they say, with the "big red team" as the Maroons were sometimes called. He took a few practice shots at goalkeeper Lorne Chabot during the warm-ups, and he stood at centre ice while the band played "God Save the King" (the King who would soon take it on the lam with Mrs. Windsor). He probably played a shift or two, reminded before he jumped over the boards to "Watch yourself out there, young fellah!"

After the Rangers game on Tuesday night, the dressing room is crowded with reporters and well-wishers, hangers-on. Here is steam and sweat and smoke enough for a legion of warriors. Men in fedoras with overcoats on their arms have fired up cigarettes and stogies and are slapping backs and asking questions. Scribbling replies on notepads. T. P. Gorman always has a word for the press: "But we're in a hurry, boys. There's a train to catch." And trying to get past all these people to the showers can be a chore for a man holding a towel around his waist.

"Excuse me, bub!" And examining an ugly-looking welt under your ribs can provoke mild outrage.

"Will you look at what that son of a bitch did to me! Fucking butt-end. Right in front of the man's eyes and he never called it. Christ, it was as plain as the nose on your face."

"Oh, stop your gabbing and get out of my way. I got a bigger bruise than that on my dick."

"That was quite the scrap you had with Coulter, Lionel."

"How did Toronto do tonight?"

"They lost 3-2."

"Fucking A-okay!"

"Well, you and Heller sure aren't in love with one another, eh, Hooley!"

"Come on now, boys! Move it along!"

"Don't get your bowels in an uproar, boss! I'm nearly ready."

The team is in a good mood. They have been playing well lately and are now tied with Toronto for first place in their division. The players feel confident that they can repeat as Stanley Cup champions. There are plenty of wisecracks as men attach garters to stockings and pull on suit pants, snapping braces over shoulders and buttoning vests. Brushes flatten hair and clothes are stuffed into bags. "Okay, okay, I'm coming." And if you are a raw rookie who has been among these men for only three days, you keep your mouth shut unless you are spoken to, and even then you say as little as possible. In the corridor outside the dressing room, Tommy Gorman has the last word.

"Sorry boys. No more questions. We've got to catch a train."

The train again! But if you played professional hockey in the 1930s, you had to get used to the train or find another line of work. And who would call this work anyway? Sitting around smoking and playing hearts! Like a sailor at sea, you get used to things: you touch the backs of the seats for balance as you make your way through the coaches to the dining car; you allow for the sideways shift on curves as you deal a card or fork a boiled potato into your mouth. In the middle of the night you can miss the bowl entirely and piss on your foot on some of those curves. And what is all this stopping and starting for anyway? From behind berth curtains come groggy voices.

"What time is it?"

"Two o'clock."

"Where are we?"

"How the fuck should I know? Go to sleep!"

"We're at Brockville, assholes. You should know that by now."

On the other side of the window, brakemen in raincoats wave lanterns back and forth, and sometimes you seem to be backing up for hours. At 8:35 this train arrives in Toronto: "Union Station! Downtown Toronto! Union Station! Stay aboard please for Hamilton, London, Windsor, Detroit and Chicago!"

Chicago! "Hog Butcher for the World," "City of the Big Shoulders," as the poet put it. Turf of legendary gangsters and big-time butter-and-egg men. And stiff from hours in the dry, smoky air of the coach, you step down to the platform for a whiff of the windy city's sooty air on this cool grey evening.

"All right now, boys, four to a taxi and we'll see you at the hotel."

And my goodness, look at all these lights! Isn't this a naughty place! *Girls, Girls, Girls. Beer and Liquor for Sale. The Best Steak in Town. Right Here! Appearing Now, Six of New York's Loveliest Show Girls!* And looking out the taxi window two players exchange a word or two.

"Would you say that a young man like Mr. Wheeler could get into trouble on a street like this?"

"I wouldn't be at all surprised. We'll have to keep an eye on him."

The coach calls a team meeting in his room. He wants to remind everybody that tomorrow night's game will be one of the most important of the season.

"You don't want to start looking past tomorrow night to Saturday, boys. That game with the Leafs will take care of itself in due course. It's tomorrow night's game that matters now and the Black Hawks will be tough. They always are. Remember, we've each won two this year. This is the rubber. In your room tonight by eleven. No later. I mean that. Practice tomorrow at ten."

But the Maroons are a veteran team. To a man they know the importance of the next night's game. Tommy's spiel is just part of his job. A roomful of hockey players in vests and shirtsleeves in a Chicago hotel room on an evening in March 1936. And the young blond-haired man at the back of the room near one of the windows is my father. The following day he writes my mother on hotel stationery.

HOTEL OMEGA
23355 STATE STREET
CHICAGO, ILLINOIS
LE 7415

Thursday, March 12, 1936

Dear Gracie:

Well, here I am in Chicago. It sure is a big city but I haven't had much of a chance to see it. We got in last night. Boy, is that ever a long train ride from Montreal. It's now one o'clock in the afternoon and this morning we had a practice at the Chicago Stadium. Most of the fellows are now sleeping or playing cards. We have our dinner at three o'clock and then we have a big game tonight with the Chicago team. I think they will give us a good fight tonight. I played a little in the two games in Montreal. Mr. Gorman told me this morning that he might try me tonight with Bob Gracie and Herb Cain. They are two swell guys and terrific players. Well, everybody is a really good player on this team. You really have to be, I guess, and please don't think I'm boasting. After the game it's on to Toronto where we play on Saturday night and that game will be on the radio, so maybe you could listen to it. Imagine that, Gracie! Me on the radio. Just like Amos "N" Andy (ha ha). The boys are a

swell bunch and a lot of fun. They are always playing jokes. This morning in the hotel dining room
some of them played a joke on this young couple
who are on their honeymoon. It was funny but I
felt kind of sorry for the young woman because she
was so embarrased. Did I spell that right? I've never
seen anybody's face so red. She had to leave the dining room. Honest to goodness, the boys will do
anything for a laugh. Well, I have to go now. I'll get
a stamp and put this in the mailbox. They have one
in the lobby downstairs. Don't forget to wish me
luck in tonight's game and on Saturday too in
Toronto. I guess by the time you get this letter those
games will be over and done with. But I think you
know what I mean. Give the baby a hug for me, and
if you get a chance, say hello to Mildred for me.

Your loving husband,

Ross

What was the joke that turned the young woman's face so
red and caused her to flee from the hotel dining room? The
couple were on their honeymoon. How did he know that,
I wonder? So the joke obviously had something to do with
sex, and a young couple's honeymoon in Chicago was
marred. But by what we shall never know. What we do
know is that on Thursday, March 12, 1936, according to
the Montreal *Gazette*, "the Maroons played one of their

best games of the season, coming from behind to tie the Black Hawks 3-3." Here is the scoring summary of that game.

First Period
Chicago — Seibert, March, Thompson 18.40
Chicago — Gottselig, March, Seibert 19.30

Second Period
Montreal — Trottier, Blinco 9.40
Chicago — Levinsky, Brydson 11.15
Montreal — Northcott, Ward, Smith 18.30

Third Period
Montreal — Cain, Marker, Gracie 5.30

Overtime
No scoring

No mention of Buddy Wheeler.

CHARLES PETTINGER'S *new untitled novel is a long and ambitious undertaking, the work of twenty years. The book chronicles the life of Will Ready who is born on January 1, 1900. Ready becomes, if you like, a personification of the century, celebrating its triumphs, suffering its calamities, a witness to . . .*

After an absence of twenty years from the publishing scene, Charles Pettinger has submitted this massive novel (about 300,000 words). It appears to be the work of a lifetime, an enormous and courageous attempt at a synthesis . . .

I can remember the excitement around Caedmon House twenty-three years ago when The Rage of the Freeway Driver *came over the transom. Those of us who read the manuscript recognized at once the fresh comic voice in those stories, a voice that so perfectly articulated the absurdities . . .*

As a narrative, this novel, I'm afraid, just doesn't work. The characters have no life. They are merely spokespersons(????) for positions taken by the author in his heroic attempt to satirize our century's excesses. The book is not really a novel at all; it is a lecture, a diatribe, a long and mostly unfunny complaint about our unwillingness as a species to behave reasonably. I agree with every scolding syllable of it, but that is hardly sufficient reason for recommending publication . . .

I am spared from completing these miserable observations by the telephone's ringing, and hanging on to the banister, an aging man with a damaged heart, I make my careful descent to the front hallway. On the other end of the line is Linda Macklin. Her mood has altered for the better since last we spoke, though I find her cheerful, booming voice disheartening. Linda is always at her worst when she seems the most buoyant. I call it her smiles-and-knives mood.

"Howard? Linda here! How are you feeling?"

"Quite good, thank you. I think I'm ready to come back to work. As a matter of fact, I'm going to have a word with my doctor about that."

"Don't rush anything, Howard! Your health is a lot more important than anything we're doing around here."

We both pause to consider this transparent falsehood.

"Howard! The reason I phoned. Have you finished the Pettinger thing?"

"Just about, yes." Why, I wonder, do I want to forestall this?

"I take it then that you've read enough for an opinion?"

"Well, yes. But, Linda, I don't like to rush a judgement. The man has put a score of years into this book."

Linda's burst of laughter may be accurately described as a guffaw.

"'A score of years!' I like that, Howard. You're sounding almost biblical this morning."

I have no idea why I used that old-fashioned noun unless it was Pettinger's influence. There are eloquent moments in that book. Pettinger has read his Bible and *Book of Common Prayer*.

"What I'm saying, Linda . . ."

"What you're saying, Howard, is let's be nice to the man and let him down gently. But the manuscript doesn't have it. Right?"

"Well, certainly it's not as good as I would have hoped."

Linda chuckles at my feeble defence.

"Not as good as you would have hoped. Howard, it's a disaster. Pure and simple, a disaster."

She sounds quite merry about all this.

"Then I take it that you've read it too?" I say.

Though how could that be? She phoned me one afternoon to say that the manuscript had just arrived and she was sending it by courier that day; indeed it arrived the next morning. She couldn't possibly have read it that night.

"I glanced at it, Howard," Linda says. "We all did that afternoon. We were like a bunch of kids opening a Christmas present. Naturally we were all curious to see what the mystery man had done after twenty years. So we all took a peek. Alas, it was unanimous. We were all disappointed in a major way. But then I began to wonder. Maybe we were all missing something. That's why I wanted you to look at it."

They had all looked at it. That would have been Linda and her two assistant editors, a salesman or two, the promotion woman. Was the courier man looking over someone's shoulder too? Poor Pettinger! I realize attention spans have shrunk drastically in the past twenty years, but this was ridiculous. Yet I feel suddenly ridiculous myself, hopelessly antiquated and irrelevant.

"Listen, Howard," continues Linda. "Pettinger phoned again yesterday. He's coming into town on Friday, and I remember your telling me last time we talked that you had to come in for a doctor's appointment." She pauses. "Could you be an angel and take the man out to lunch and give him the news? A huge favour, Howard."

"Don't you first want to see my report on the manuscript?"

"For the record, yes. Just send me a page or two. Details aren't necessary. After all, you're just confirming our opinion."

"But I'm wondering," I say, "shouldn't you tell the man? After all, you're editorial director, Linda. Pettinger has been on our list for over twenty years."

"I would, Howard, but the fact is I can't. I'll be in New York on Friday. Leaving at sunrise, I'm afraid."

"I see."

"What time is your doctor's appointment?"

"Eleven o'clock."

"Good! Where do you think our man would like to eat?"

"Del Shannon used to take him to the Park Plaza, as I recall."

"The Prince Arthur Room! Perfect! I'll book a table for one o'clock. Will that give you enough time?"

"You don't want to discuss this at an editorial meeting? It seems a rather summary way to deal with a writer who has meant a great deal to our reputation as a literary house over the years."

"Howard, be fair! Think of the times we have to work in. You know and I know that the manuscript would require a major editorial overhaul. Months of work! And we'd still have a big, sleepy dog on our hands. The unit cost would be catastrophic. And Pettinger is no spring chicken. He must be pushing sixty. How many more books does he have in him?"

"Only one more at this rate, I suppose. If he lives to be eighty . . ."

"My point exactly. Okay, I have his phone number here. Can you give him a call and invite him to lunch on Friday? Do you have a pen handy?"

I grope in mother's secretary, pulling out the little drawers that once held bills and receipts and find a pen. When I scratch the back of an old cheque-book, the pen appears to be dried out, but it finally yields a little ink, and I write down Pettinger's number.

"Howard, I appreciate this. Phone me next Monday and let me know how things went."

"Of course."

"Thanks again, Howard. Take care now."

"Yes. Take care."

No hint of when I am to come back or indeed if I am to be

invited back at all. Will I have to take my daughter's advice and talk to a lawyer and go through all that dreary business?

The thought of it is so dispiriting. Standing by the front door, I look through the panes of coloured glass at the Sold sign hammered into the front lawn yesterday afternoon by Mrs. Chernyk. I decide to postpone my call to Charles Pettinger. I'll try him later in the afternoon, before dinner, when perhaps he has had a drink or two to dull the day's bitter edge. But then I remember that Pettinger no longer drinks; at one point in his life alcohol nearly ruined his marriage.

THE LATE WINTER OF 1936 was wet and many rivers in eastern North America overflowed their banks. Towns along these rivers were under water, and in the newspapers of the day are pictures of families in rowboats on the streets of Belleville, Ontario, or stranded on the roofs of their houses in Johnstown, Pennsylvania. But no river flows through Huron Falls; there is Little Lake at one end and Georgian Bay at the other, and while the water was high, it posed no threat to the town.

On the afternoon of Saturday, March 14, people looked out their windows at the grey rain and thought perhaps of spring. If they were interested in hockey, they looked forward to listening to the game that night from Maple Leaf Gardens between the Montreal Maroons and the Toronto Maple Leafs. Even Leaf fans in the town were pulling for Buddy Wheeler; after all, he was one of them and he had made it to the National Hockey League. Thursday's edition of the *Huron Falls Times* carried a feature on Buddy Wheeler by Chip McNeil entitled "Local Hockey Star on Radio Saturday." McNeil and Leo Kennedy and George

Fowler were already on their way to Toronto, where three tickets awaited them at the Gardens, compliments of T. P. Gorman.

Would my mother listen to the game? She was asked that very question by Mr. Carey who came by each Saturday morning with his parcels of sausages and pork chops. The butcher was mindful of the dirty water he had tracked into the kitchen, for Mrs. Wheeler was a fussy young woman.

"I suppose," he says, "you'll be listening to that hockey match tonight, Mrs. Wheeler?"

"I suppose I will, Mr. Carey," my mother says, opening her purse, "but I'm not really much of a hockey enthusiast."

Enthusiast! I imagine the butcher thinking something along the lines of "My aren't we fancy though!" as he searches for change in the big leather pouch on his belt.

All her life Mother would either amuse or infuriate her neighbours by using words that small-town folk considered unnecessary. As a child I could detect their resentment when mother would agree that it was indeed a fine day by saying something like, "Yes, the weather is very agreeable, isn't it?"

People thought she was putting on airs when in fact she was only trying to vary her vocabulary in the interests of self-improvement. She took seriously the *Reader's Digest*'s "It Pays to Increase Your Word Power," and during the summer of my twelfth year, for one awful month, she insisted that we play a game requiring each of us to use a new word every day.

"Well, anyhow," says Mr. Carey, "it's a great thing for your husband to play with the professionals like that."

"I suppose it is. Thank you, Mr. Carey."

"Thank *you*, Mrs. Wheeler," says the butcher, touching his cap and descending the steps to walk along the side of the house. "Enthusiast! Well, well, well!"

I remember Mr. Carey years later as a large, amiable man who was often laughing and wagging his great, bald head as though unable to contain his mirth at the comic antics of his fellow humans.

Towards the end of this wet, dark afternoon, while my mother prepares a boiled potato and pork chop for her dinner, an old Chevy pulls up in front of the house. The driver keeps the motor running and you can hear its thin clatter all along the street. Only one of the headlamps is working. The car is filled with people who have to turn this way and that to allow Mildred Wheeler to climb out. During the exercise there is much laughter and tomfoolery, and no one would be surprised to learn that a bottle of liquor is being passed around. Even after eight hours on her feet at Woolworth's, Mildred still has energy enough to run along the front walk and up the veranda steps. When my mother comes to the front door holding the baby, Mildred is beside herself with excitement.

"Grace! There's a party at our house. Come along! We're all going to listen to the game later. If you say you'll come, I'll go out and tell Eddie and then he'll come back for us. We have a car full right now."

Mother always disliked surprises. You dropped in on her unannounced at your peril. One clear spring Sunday, many years later, I took Gillian and the children for a drive in the country. We explored the backroads of central Ontario and, by the middle of the afternoon, found ourselves within thirty miles of "Grandma's house." Mother hadn't seen us in months, but I could tell that she wasn't exactly thrilled by our sudden appearance on her doorstep.

"You might have phoned, Howard," was the whispered reproach while I helped her make the sandwiches and tea. Spontaneity was not a part of her nature; a matter of adjusting her sights, I suppose. Like Eliot's Prufrock, she needed time "To prepare a face to meet the faces that you meet."

And now here she was with her meal already on the stove. No, it was entirely out of the question.

"I already have my dinner on the stove, Mildred."

"Oh, come on, Grace. It'll be fun. Aren't you going to listen to the game?"

"I expect I will, yes."

"I'll look after the baby," says Mildred, holding out her arms for the child. She has kicked off her rubbers and now dances around the front hallway singing "You are my sunshine, my only sunshine."

It was Aunt Mildred's favourite song for years. She and her sisters sang it together at family parties, and until I was five or six, she always sang or hummed it when she rocked me. From the street comes the sound of the Chevy's horn, and Grace imagines the neighbours parting curtains to peer out at this ruckus in front of the Wheeler house. Mildred hands over the baby and puts on her rubbers.

"Are you sure you won't join us, Grace?"

"No thanks, Mildred. I'm fine right here."

And so she is, with her boiled potato and pork chop and *Star Weekly*.

The Montreal Maroons have arrived in Toronto one point behind the Maple Leafs and unbeaten in their last six games. But they are a tired and bruised team, with Robinson, Lamb and now Gus Marker unable to play. Their best centre, Hooley Smith, is "nursing a sore groin," though Tommy Gorman tells the Toronto press that "the Hooler will play. You won't keep that man out of the game." As for the Maple Leafs, they are confident. They believe that they are the better team. They also have two games in hand and will play the Maroons twice within the next week. The Leafs are also still smarting from a year ago when they were expected to win the Stanley Cup but were thrashed in three straight by the Montreal club. Their owner, Connie Smythe, has not let his players or their fans forget that, and on this Saturday night, 14,586, the largest crowd ever to watch a hockey game in Maple Leaf Gardens, jams the arena on Carlton Street. On the radio, from his gondola high above the ice, Foster Hewitt describes the action.

At the Wheeler house on Dock Street, Buddy's friends eat ham sandwiches and drink Old Stock Ale, waiting for Hewitt to mention Buddy's name. Where the hell is he anyway? Why hasn't Gorman put him on the ice? He's short of right-wingers, isn't he? He's already double-shifting Ward. He'll wear the man out, for Christ's sake. The game is a scoreless tie until midway through the second period when the Maroons' Dave Trottier lifts what looks like a harmless backhander towards the Toronto net. In front of fourteen and a half thousand pairs of disbelieving eyes, the puck eludes Toronto goalkeeper George Hainsworth and skids into the net. As one sports writer put it in his account of the game, "George had time for a cup of tea before the puck actually reached him." The big Toronto crowd falls silent and glum. The Maroons are a defensive team, skilful and dogged when it comes to protecting a lead. It seems that every time they get the puck, they just dump it into the Toronto end. The Leafs look increasingly frustrated. Towards the end of the second period, the revellers on Dock Street hear Buddy Wheeler's name for the first time.

"Shut up everybody. He's on the ice now."

"About goddamn time."

"Shut up!"

"Come on now, Buddy! Show them your stuff!"

"Will ya *please* shut up?"

In this house Grace has put the baby to bed and now sits in the rocking chair by the kitchen window reading the *Star Weekly*. She is thinking that within the next two weeks she must mention spring-cleaning to Violet. She has noticed too that this persistent rain has weakened the eaves on the south side of the house, and they will need repair. Perhaps Mr. Ball can recommend a reliable man. The hockey game is turned down on the radio; she can just make out Hewitt's high-pitched voice as he describes a game that she has never been interested in nor understood. She finds it mildly intriguing, however, that her husband is now paid to play hockey, though it seems to her a frivolous way to earn your daily bread.

Still, he sends money home, and money is always welcome. Money is a comfort, no two ways about that. Just try living without it and see how far you get. Money keeps a roof over your head, and thank God for this house and the baby's health, and this precious hold on whatever good fortune we may briefly possess, for it can all perish as swiftly as fire consumes grass or water a drowning child. At twenty-four, Grace has already accepted the transitory nature of happiness and the vanity of human wishes. Man proposes, but God disposes. It is the doctrine she will hear expounded next morning at Knox Church.

When Grace hears her husband's name on the radio, she reaches over and gives the volume knob a quarter turn.

> "Four minutes left now in the second period and the Montreal Maroons are leading the Leafs one to nothing on a strange goal by Trottier at 11:15 of this period. The play looked innocent enough. Russ Blinco passed the puck across to Trottier who seemed to be leaving the ice as he lobbed the puck into the Leaf end. It appeared to hit something in front of the net and, changing direction, went in. Hainsworth seemed just as surprised as everyone else . . . in any case, the Maroons are ahead by a goal as the teams change players. The Leafs now have Joe Primeau with Harvey Jackson and Charlie Conacher on the wings. Horner and Clancy are on the defence. The Maroons have Smith at centre with Northcott on the left side and rookie Buddy

Wheeler now on right wing. Tommy Gorman is giving Ward a rest . . . Jimmy Ward has played a lot of hockey tonight. Wheeler is up from the Windsor Bulldogs of the International League. A blond-haired youngster. Now taking his place alongside Hooley Smith for the face-off . . . The draw goes to Primeau who knocks the puck into the Montreal end. Harvey Jackson moving in along the boards. Being watched there by Wentworth. Now Stuart Evans has the puck behind his own net. Shoots it off the boards to Northcott. Baldy Northcott stick-handling out of his own end with Smith and Wheeler to centre ice. Northcott shoots the puck into the Leaf end . . . And that's what the Maroons have been doing most of this game. The Leafs sometimes look a little frustrated by all this. The Maroons are checking them tightly and the Leafs can't seem to get anything started. Now Clancy has the puck. Across to Charlie Conacher. The big right-winger comes to centre ice. Being bothered there by Northcott . . . he gets away from North-cott. Passes over to Jackson. Back to Conacher. Here is Conacher coming in now. He shoots . . . Chabot makes the save. A good one. That's the best chance the Leafs have had this period . . . Primeau now with the puck behind the Montreal net. A pass out. Intercepted by Evans . . . Evans to Smith. Hooley Smith stickhandling to centre ice. A pass to Wheeler. Wheeler into the Leafs' zone. Checked along the boards by Horner . . . Smith and Horner with their sticks up in front of Hainsworth . . . and Clancy clears the puck out of the Leaf end. Now Wheeler and Northcott battling Jackson along the boards. Northcott comes up with the puck. Ragging the puck now . . . Waiting for Smith to come out. Now he gets it over to Smith. Smith attacking again with Wheeler . . . And the whistle goes. Wheeler . . . a little too eager got in ahead of the play and it's offside . . . Now Jimmy Ward is coming on the ice for the Maroons. He's had his breather. Ward gives the youngster a tap on the legs with his stick as Wheeler leaves the ice. Ward now on right wing with Smith and Northcott. And Tommy Gorman is also sending out Lionel Conacher and Allan Shields on defence . . ."

Everyone in Huron Falls who is listening to this game waits attentively for Foster Hewitt to mention Buddy Wheeler's name again. But, in fact, Buddy Wheeler's days as a big leaguer are over. His journey to the New American Hotel has already begun in the dressing room after the game when a jubilant Tommy Gorman claps him on the back and says, "Nice work, young fellah, but I'm going to have to let you go home for a while." Gorman really has no choice in the matter as he explains, "Earl and Joe and Gus will all be coming back next week, and you're not quite ready to take their place, son. We're going to send you some money."

"Hey, Tommy," yells a reporter from across the room. "What did you think of Trottier's goal?"

Tommy Gorman pats Buddy one more time on the back and gets to his feet.

"It went in, didn't it? That's all I care about. Didn't I tell you guys we could handle Toronto? And we'll beat them again Tuesday night too. These boys of mine are on their way to another Stanley Cup."

But it was not to be. In two weeks the Maroons will enter the playoffs against Detroit and go down in three straight games. In two years, they will be finished. Out of business. As the decade draws to a close, the city of Montreal can support only one hockey team and the Canadiens will be the survivor. On this Saturday night in March 1936, though, the Maroons are in first place in their division, and outside their dressing room in Maple Leaf Gardens, T. P. Gorman, gripping Buddy Wheeler's elbow, has a word with George Fowler. Gorman is in a hurry and has to raise his voice above the hubbub in the corridor.

"Listen, George, I like this boy. He's got some good moves, and he's been a real help to us over the past week. But I can't find a place for him on the team right now. Earl will soon be back and Joe Lamb and Gus Marker too. I have to go with our regulars. I'm sure you can understand that. But say, I want to see this young fellow at our training camp next fall. All right? We'll send him a ticket. Now I have to run. Good talking to you, George."

When it is all over, you can only go home. According to the rules of the day, a player called up to the NHL had to wait twenty-one days before he could return to his original club. By Saturday, March 14, the Windsor team's season was nearly over. There was nothing to do but go home. Climb into the back seat of the LaSalle next to Chip McNeil and go home. And driving north from the city in the big car, the four men in their overcoats and hats could pass for gangsters. Buddy is only half-listening as Leo Kennedy, without turning around, says, "They didn't give you enough time out there, Buddy."

Over Leo Kennedy's shoulder, Buddy can see the round yellow light of the speedometer and George Fowler's homburg and fur-collared coat, the gloved hands on the steering wheel.

"Now let's be fair, Leo," says Fowler. "Tommy did his best. That was a big game for them."

From his corner Chip McNeil turns his comically mournful face towards Buddy. "I thought you did okay, Bud, but like Leo says, they only gave you that one shift."

McNeil looks out his window. "By God, that Jimmy Ward is a fine player, isn't he?"

"You're right about that, Chip," says Leo Kennedy. "Ward is a humdinger."

"What a crowd they put in there tonight!" says McNeil. "My God, I've never seen so many people under one roof. I'll bet old Conn Smythe must have been raking it in tonight, eh, George?"

For his own reasons, George Fowler finds McNeil's remark provoking. Fowler may be a little touchy because his protégé did not stay with the big club, but he is also a little put out from time to time with the company that he is now obliged to keep. Who is McNeil anyway to talk about a man like Conn Smythe? McNeil is just a small-town scribbler. A dime-a-dozen sportswriter and a soaker to boot. In the rear-view mirror Fowler surveys Chip McNeil's long drinker's face and hound-dog eyes.

"Yes, I expect it was a profitable evening for Conn," says Fowler. "Do you have any objections to a man making money, Chip? Do you see something wrong with that?"

McNeil can detect the rancour in Fowler's voice.

"Not at all, George. It was just an observation."

But Fowler won't let go of this and glances across at Leo Kennedy.

"You don't suppose, Leo, that our newspaper friend in the back seat is really a Red, do you?"

Leo Kennedy is only too eager to play the game.

"Could be, George. Could be."

Fowler again looks in the mirror.

"You believe in what the Communists say, do you, Chip? A man should not be allowed to make a profit. Is that it?"

Chip McNeil doesn't like George Fowler. How could anyone like the fat son of a bitch? On the other hand, Chip McNeil does like the fact that the Huron House is right across the street from the newspaper office. It would be a shame not to feel welcome at the hotel when noon hour arrives. And then Fowler owns the hockey and softball teams. If he wished to, he could make Chip McNeil's job difficult.

"I am certainly no Communist, George. I can assure you of that, my friend. As for Mr. Smythe, he's entitled to every penny he can get. And by the way, that's a great arena he's built. Great place to watch a game!"

This is followed by silence and finally Chip McNeil takes a leather-covered flask from a pocket of his overcoat. After a decorous sip, he offers the flask to Buddy.

"Like a snort, Bud? Canadian Club?"

"I don't mind," says Buddy, taking a long drink. He can feel the whisky travelling through him and warming his blood. He feels tired but happy. Playing in front of all those people tonight is something he will never forget. He didn't stay with the team, but he did play four games with them. He did something that not one in ten thousand guys will ever do. And he has been invited to training camp in the fall.

From the front seat comes the soft rumble of Leo Kennedy's voice. "I wouldn't say no to a pull from that flask, Chipper, old chum?"

"Right you are, Leo."

After he drinks Kennedy says, "How about you, George?"

All evening Fowler has felt a burgeoning contempt for his companions. In the Gardens, they were like schoolboys who had never been to the city before. What rubes they are! Now he feels like asking Kennedy if he thinks he is talking to another country dummy who drinks whisky at the wheel of an expensive car. But he doesn't. The fact is that he now has to do business every day of his life with the likes of these people. So he only smiles.

"Thank you, no, Leo."
Leo Kennedy rests the flask on top of his fedora.
"Bud? Another?"
"Sure."

I AM SOMETHING of a coward, nervous and conciliatory before difficult people. My father was like this too, but he was able to charm those who might resist him. It was his single slender gift from the gods after his hockey playing days were over, and it enabled him to sell used Buicks for a living. Unfortunately I had a timid, serious manner. I could not tell a funny story and I had inherited my mother's sturdy reluctance to join anything resembling a group. This was a drawback in my early days in publishing when I was a sales representative, and so I was enormously relieved when I was transferred to the editorial department. There I could close the door and read and edit manuscripts. My wife used to complain that I was always reading, "hiding," as she put it, "behind other people's words." It was a valid judgement.

Editors, however, have to meet people from time to time and, in my early years, I could be especially intimidated by writers with reputations for being ornery. We once had a poet on our list, a one-season wonder whose erotic verse captured a fleeting popularity. He was an unpleasant character, supercilious and derisive, and his brief notoriety went completely to his head. One day Del Shannon invited me to lunch with him and the poet. Throughout the meal the man mercilessly cut me; as far as he was concerned, I wasn't even there. It was a remarkable display of unrelieved rudeness, and later Del acknowledged that the poet had been an ass, "but we must stroke and keep blithe the spirits of these insufferable writing types, dear boy." Del was superb at that. I used to watch him at cocktail parties, hoping to learn how to be suave and sophisticated. But I did not have the gift; I was neither witty nor prepossessing, and so I continued to stumble among strangers.

Charles Pettinger was nothing like the poet, but he was nevertheless a formidable presence. Something austere and patrician about him invited a cautious approach. No one would easily address him as Chuck or Charlie. Scion of an old Boston family, he had come to Canada during the Vietnam War. His age and family connections would have kept him out of it, but like many of his fellow countrymen at the time, he was protesting the entire American experience in the Far East. By doing so, he alienated his family, or so Del told me. Handsome and tall and stoop-shouldered, he carried himself like a man for whom each doorway was a hazard. An authentic misanthropist, he had a fund of stories, all of which had to do with the inveterate foolishness of the world. A story by Pettinger was like a walnut in the jaws of a nutcracker. You eventually got the meat, and it was nourishing, but you were also aware that a certain violence had been committed.

In the days following the publication of his first book, a visit to the office by Pettinger created a stir. People would say to one another, "Charles Pettinger is coming in this afternoon." My office adjoined Del Shannon's, and he often kept his door open, for he loved to shock the secretaries when he told visitors tales of his amorous adventures in the bathhouses of New York. From my desk I could see Pettinger's long legs crossed at the ankles, the elegant leather boots. In those days he dressed like an English landed gent in corduroy suits and trilby hats. Sometimes I would hear him complaining of the cultural aridity of country life: the absence of neighbours who read anything of value; the tedium of the school play he was obliged to attend, since his wife directed it.

Jane Pettinger taught English at the local high school and was their primary source of income. I remember her as a plain, calm, dark-haired young woman who was extremely hospitable during my visit to their farmhouse. She had been educated at one of the Toronto girls' schools, and later at Victoria College where she took classes from Northrop Frye. Margaret Atwood had been a classmate. Robert Browning was Jane Pettinger's poetic interest and she knew a great deal about the man and his work. Jane wore skirts and cashmere sweaters, and I could see her reading "My Last Duchess" to farmers' sons, undismayed by their blank responses. In the early years of their marriage she had also to contend with her husband's drinking, and with the ladies who inevitably appear at readings in the public libraries and university common rooms.

Many years ago I had to attend an academic conference at Queen's University and Del Shannon gave me the job of delivering a parcel of books to Pettinger at his farm an hour's drive from Kingston. "A chance to see the great man at his hearth" was how Del put it. It was a cold grey afternoon in late November, a day for whisky by the fire. Out on the country roads, I was relieved to be away at last from the professors with their prattle about texture in Virginia Woolf and something or other in T. S. Eliot. The red letters on the mailbox said simply Pettinger. As I drove down the laneway, a golden retriever bounded along the farmyard, and a tall figure came out the kitchen door. He was dressed in cord pants with a flannel shirt and one of those down-filled vests worn by hunters. The retriever was an amiable creature and tugged me gently forward by covering my hand with its wet mouth. Pettinger was cordiality itself; the iciness he often displayed in Toronto had vanished. Of course he had been drinking. It was only four o'clock, but already his face was flushed.

"Come in and have a drink! How is Del?"

I sat at the kitchen table. The house smelled of wood smoke and the dog. I looked around while Pettinger made drinks at the counter from a bottle of Cutty Sark. In this house he had written *The Rage of the Freeway Driver*, and was now just finishing *Unholy Wars*. People were eagerly awaiting its appearance. Ahead of him lay adversity and disappointment: lukewarm reviews and alcoholic brooding; twenty years in the woods at a task that would yield nothing. On that darkening November afternoon, however,

Pettinger was in good spirits as he stroked the dog's large silky head and swallowed his Cutty Sark. We had a second drink.

"Let me show you the place," he said.

There was a workshop with power tools in the basement. Pettinger was restoring a cabinet that the previous owners had painted a ghastly mauve. "Barbarians," said Pettinger. I was surprised to discover this side of him; I had always thought that men of letters were unhandy. Upstairs in his study, I could see through a large window across the fields and laneway to the township road. "My eyrie," said Pettinger. "My retreat from the world."

I looked at the great slab of wood upon which he wrote and the heavy grey typewriter. Next to it was a yellow legal pad and a jar full of pencils and a neat pile of manuscript pages. Pettinger stood behind, waiting for me to admire his workplace. And I did. It looked like the ideal spot for an intelligent and perceptive observer of the times to order his thoughts and transcribe them for grateful readers. Beyond the window we could see a yellow school bus moving along the road and behind it a station wagon turning into the laneway.

"Here comes Jane now," said Pettinger. "Let's go down and hear all about how the farmers' sons don't appreciate Browning."

Jane Pettinger seemed glad to have company. Like many city people who decide to live in isolated surroundings, she was talkative with guests, and I sensed that despite her obvious love and respect for Pettinger, she felt a bit oppressed. It was not hard to see why: cooped up each night while her husband drank or sanded cabinets in the basement or brooded over his book. Such a life requires loyalty and stamina, and even then it must get to you. I liked Jane Pettinger, and when she pressed me to stay for dinner, I accepted.

She talked about Browning and the thesis she had set aside when Pettinger entered her life. One day she would resume her studies, but now Charles's writing was more important than her doctorate. Pettinger accepted the compliment in silence. Perhaps he had heard it all before and wasn't paying attention. After dinner he grew rather glum, sitting on the sofa with a glass of Cutty Sark in hand, staring at the fire. It struck me that he had a daily quota of goodwill for visitors, and I had now used it up; his gloomy countenance seemed to say, "Please bugger off!" Driving back to Kingston through a windy, dark night, I thought of Jane Pettinger marking papers at the dining-room table while her husband refilled his glass and stared into the fire. And dialling Pettinger's number over twenty years later, I wonder if she is now just arriving home in another station wagon after another day teaching *Macbeth* or *Lord of the Flies*. Walking into the kitchen and calling for him. Wondering what frame of mind he is in this afternoon. That long dark hair must be grey by now.

The phone rings several times before I hear his voice.

"Yes?" The voice sounds wary, even hostile; it is the voice of a man who has been importuned once too often by the carpet-cleaning people. *What is it now?*

"Charles Pettinger? It's Howard Wheeler of Caedmon

House. We met many years ago. In fact, I came out to your place once."

His tone changes and becomes surprisingly friendly.

"Of course. Yes, I remember. You worked with Del Shannon. I remember your visit. You brought me some books. That was a long time ago."

"Yes, it was."

I know what he is waiting for. He is waiting for glad tidings. For confirmation that twenty years of work is now going to be rewarded with approval and success. *We love your book. New York does too. We think it's going to be a huge hit.*

"Linda Macklin has told me that you are coming to town this Friday," I say. "I wonder, would you happen to be free for lunch?"

"Why yes, I am. That would be nice."

"How about the Park Plaza at one o'clock?"

I hear what sounds like a soft chuckle.

"The old Plaza? Is it still in business? I haven't been there for years. Remember the old song, 'Don't Get Around Much Any More'?"

"It's still there," I say. "The Prince Arthur Room?"

"Fine."

"I expect we'll be able to recognize one another without difficulty."

"I'm sure we will."

There is a moment of clumsy silence when neither of us seems able to finish this.

"Well, I'll see you on Friday then, Mr. Pettinger."

"All right, Mr. Wheeler. Thanks for calling."

He doesn't sound much like the Pettinger of old with his patrician manner and sardonic tales. He sounds more like a man holding on to a lifeline and looking around for help. He seemed more his old remote self when I saw him last year at Del Shannon's funeral. He arrived alone and sat by himself at the back of the chapel, an elderly countryman in a tweed suit with a Tilley hat in his lap. He looked stern and unapproachable, alone with his memories of Del. The cemetery chapel was filled with book-trade people: publishers, authors, newspaper and magazine writers. Yet no one recognized Pettinger; he was a forgotten man.

At the graveside on that bright and windy June day he spoke briefly to Del's mother, a handsome woman in her eighties. In the aftermath of a storm, the northwest wind was all around us, rushing through the new leaves of the trees, pressing Mrs. Shannon's dress against her legs. She had to keep a hand on her wide black hat and veil while she received Pettinger's condolences. Overhead enormous white clouds were hurrying across the city towards Lake Ontario. Later I watched Pettinger walking swiftly away among the gravestones towards the iron gates on Parliament Street, a tall, stooped figure leaning into the wind, like a man striding across a field with his dog.

WHEN A MAN RETURNS HOME after consorting with the gods, he is entitled to a reprieve from the daily grind. He cannot be expected to soil his hands with the ordinary business of living. For a while at least, he can forgo earning his daily bread: sleep late, eat a leisurely breakfast and stroll downtown to be recognized as a returning hero. He can spend an hour in the Royal Café drinking coffee, and be at the Huron House by noon when the first draft is pulled. In small towns like Huron Falls, there are always other men who want to hear what it was like to play hockey in Maple Leaf Gardens or spend a night in a Chicago hotel.

It is not as glamorous, however, for the woman who lives with such a man. She must get up at six o'clock, climbing from the warm bed where her sleeping husband smells faintly sour from last night's beer. Putting on her housecoat, she goes to the crib in the corner of the room and changes the baby's sodden diaper. When he is clean and sprinkled with talcum, she carries him downstairs, murmuring those things that mothers like to murmur to their young in the stillness of the morning before fatigue and impatience set in.

"You are getting heavier every day, my little man." She puts the child in his high chair and goes to the back kitchen for kindling to light the stove. It is April and still cool at six o'clock in the morning. While she drinks her tea and spoons oatmeal into the baby's mouth, she listens to the robins in the backyard. She is not unhappy, but she worries about her husband whose face is now mashed against the pillow, mouth open, dreaming his dreams. He will have to find something to do. This hockey business is only a flash in the pan. There is no future in playing a game.

At 6:45 Violet Day knocks on the side door and comes into the kitchen in her cloth coat and tam and heavy brown stockings, averting by habit the side of her face that is blemished. Grace has noticed a change come over Violet lately; she now seems ill at ease in the house. No longer does she hum while rocking the baby; now she looks warily about as though fearful of being watched. Grace correctly suspects that Buddy's presence in the house makes Violet nervous. She is a simple girl, easily upset by change and she is not used to having a man around the place. If he were out all day like other men, Violet could probably deal with it. This is a genuine worry for Grace; she cannot afford to lose Violet Day. Who would look after the baby while she is at Dufferin Street Public School earning their livelihood?

She thinks about this while she soaps her long pale body in the bath after breakfast. It is still on her mind as she stands in her slip in the closet choosing from half a dozen sober-coloured dresses. Buddy has burrowed beneath the covers and pulled the pillow over his head to muffle the noises of the household. When Grace leaves for school, Violet Day stands by the front door with the baby in her arms. Walking along Queen Street in the cool, fresh morning, Grace reflects that this state of affairs cannot continue. Buddy will have to find work. And he does!

George Fowler offers him a job selling cars at his lot on Bay Street. It is not hard to see Fowler's view of things. Buddy Wheeler is now a local name. He has played a few games in the National Hockey League and been invited to the Maroons' training camp in October. All summer he will be playing first base for the Huron Falls Cataracts, wearing one of their smart new grey uniforms with the maroon piping and the words "Fowler Motors" lettered across the back above the numerals. And Buddy is a personable young man. People take to him. It's good business.

For Buddy, it is the perfect job since it allows him to join the work force without radically altering his habits. He can still sleep in, for instance; nobody buys a car at eight o'clock in the morning. Now he can also drive downtown because Fowler permits the salesmen to take the machines home. So at eleven o'clock on a spring morning Buddy can step out the front door looking dapper in his slacks and glen-check jacket and fedora. After backing out the driveway, he goes down Queen Street to work, the five-year-old Hudson or Graham-Paige spurting some blue smoke into the air. Most of the cars throw a little oil after a hundred thousand miles; in fact, many of them have done service as taxis in Toronto and Hamilton and have the gearboxes to prove it.

Downtown Buddy has time to chat with his friends over coffee and toast at the Royal Café. Fowler doesn't like his salesmen drinking beer in the Huron House during office hours, but Buddy finds a way around that. He keeps a bottle of Old Dominion in the door pocket of an ancient and unsaleable Franklin rusting in the back row against the board fence. Everyone fights the quotidian blues in his own way: artists have their work and housewives their soaps; others stoke evangelical fires or buy lottery tickets to forget for a while the muddle and death that await us all. Drinkers hide bottles in strange places, swallowing a few mouthfuls from time to time throughout the day and chewing mints or sen sens to sweeten their breath.

After a few swigs, Buddy walks around the lot or sits behind one of the two varnished desks in the white wooden shack with the word Office over the door. There he shoots the breeze with Fowler's other salesman, Earl Dawes, a tall dark-complexioned man with a few strands of black hair plastered to his skull and a permanent five o'clock shadow. Dawes had an air of dissipation about him; he looked like a man who had partaken of forbidden fruits and survived, but just barely. He wore jackets with heavy padded shoulders and had a wristwatch with an expansion bracelet at a time when such accessories were uncommon in places like Huron Falls. Dawes was a man whose hands had never touched hammer or hoe; a man who would never own a house or buy life insurance. He and his wife Irma, a bleached blonde, lived in the Sundee Apartments, and spent their evenings in the Ladies and Escorts Room of the Huron House. Dawes rolled a toothpick around his mouth and had a jaunty, knowing manner. He was in fact the quintessential used-car salesman, an emblem of his trade. In later years when I would come down to the lot to see my father, Dawes always called me "Kiddo." "How are you doin', Kiddo? Want to earn two bits? Go over to the restaurant and get us some ice cream, will ya?"

Buddy and Earl do most of their business in the early evening, or on a Saturday afternoon when a farmer and his wife might drop by looking for some "economical transportation." Then Buddy parks a shoe on the bumper of a heavy old sedan and talks about mileage, while from the open doorway of the office, Earl Dawes rolls the toothpick around his mouth and looks on the proceedings with a smile, unsurprised and gratified by the world's credulity.

Three or four afternoons a week Buddy has to leave the lot early and drive home to dress for ball games. Now and then Grace comes out to watch him play, pushing the baby carriage to the ball diamond. After the game, they walk home together through the dusk with the birds settling down and neighbours talking on verandas. There is a kind of contentment to such evenings, but how can Buddy not notice the cries of teammates piling into cars for Sandy Beach? After all, he is only human, as they say. It is all very well to be on Queen Street with wife and child, but there is another kind of happiness when you are twenty-four and the apple of many eyes. And are summer nights not made for cold beer and sand-pit fires with hot dogs and corn on the cob and laughter and girls who plunge into the water in their brassieres and underpants? Is it not happiness itself to undo the straps and feel those unfamiliar breasts in your hands as you listen to the voices of friends carrying across the dark water.

> *Oh the music goes round and round*
> *Oh ho ho ho ho ho!*
> *And it comes out here!*

When Grace doesn't feel like going to a ball game, Buddy returns late, undressing quietly, leaving his uniform in a heap on the bedroom floor, smelling of beer and the bonfire and maybe another woman. Grace is beginning to wonder. Sometimes he will take her in his arms though she can sense his lack of ardour. She has no skill at lovemaking. It can't be helped. She always feels a little soiled by the experience.

This summer is not like the previous one; Buddy's resolve from the year before seems to have evaporated. This year there is no running around the cinder track at the high school, no workouts with the dumbbells in the basement. He lunches on chop suey and raisin pie at the Royal Café. In the afternoons he and Earl Dawes buy cardboard containers of ice cream which they eat in the office with little wooden paddles, their feet up on the varnished desks. There is not much exercise playing softball three times a week and Buddy grows a little paunch. He seems content enough playing ball and selling a car now and then. On bad days there is always the bottle of Old Dominion in the Franklin.

When the letter from the Maroons arrives that fall, he goes to Winnipeg without much enthusiasm. Why? Who knows? Perhaps he is too comfortable in Huron Falls. Perhaps he now realizes that he will never be good enough to stay in that league with the likes of Jimmy Ward and Hooley Smith. There have always been thousands of young men like Buddy Wheeler in small towns everywhere. Good? You bet! Listen, that boy will knock their socks off. Act? Did you see him in the school play? I just don't see how he can miss the movies some day. Did you ever hear a piano played that well? Pitch? That kid can't miss the major leagues, believe you me! Well, he can, and most likely will. Then he will have to settle for Plan B or C or D. Or no plan at all.

Two weeks after leaving for Winnipeg, Buddy is back home sporting a bruised eye. He doesn't say much about training camp and displays no desire whatsoever to spend another winter in Windsor. What is the point of playing hockey in Windsor? No point. It is back to the car lot where George Fowler now sees him in a different light. Disappointed? Of course, but these things happen. It's not the end of the world. From here on, a kind of good-natured contempt will inform Fowler's attitude towards Buddy Wheeler whom he regards as a nice guy with talent but no character. Fowler has seen scores like him and they all end up the same: salesmen or bartenders. Meantime

Buddy is useful to have around; he can sell a car, and he is still the best hockey player in these parts. In a way, too, Fowler may even be glad that Buddy Wheeler has failed. He is mean-spirited enough to believe that it will help to keep Buddy's snotty schoolteacher wife in her place.

So now Buddy plays hockey and softball for Huron Falls, and spends his days at the car lot on Bay Street. When I am old enough, seven or eight, I go with him on Saturday mornings as a treat. He lets me play in the older cars in the back row where I turn the big stiff steering wheels and try to shift the gear levers. Through the windshield I can watch my father working the customers. When I roll down the window and put out my arm as though I were driving down a highway, I can hear his pitch. And it is here in these old cars that I notice how people take to my father, in a way they will never take to my mother or to me.

The war is now on and Fowler has a lot full of cars to sell. People are working again and have money, but the problem is gasoline which is rationed to two or three gallons a week. Still folks want something to drive or even to look at in front of their houses, and since the automobile companies have stopped making cars for the marketplace, people come to my father and Earl Dawes. When I get bored playing in the cars, I walk down to the office where I can hear the drone of voices from within as my father and Dawes while away a slow afternoon playing cribbage.

"Fifteen-two, fifteen-four, fifteen-six and a pair is eight. And one for his mighty knobs."

While they play, they talk about money: about winning

the Irish Sweepstakes, about the big payoff when their ship comes in. As I listen, I understand that for them money is a way out of town, a passport to another place, a mythical, enchanted land like the one in the song my father sings while he is shaving.

> *Oh the buzzing of the bees*
> *In the cigarette trees*
> *Round the soda-water fountain.*

For my mother who sits at the little secretary in the hallway managing the household accounts, money is there to pay bills. There is no question of running anywhere because no ships are coming in and where would you run to anyway? Life has to be lived here on Queen Street in Huron Falls, Ontario, and bills and responsibilities and getting up in the morning are all a part of it.

It is about this time that my father's infidelities begin to surface, and one spring evening during the second last year of the war, there is a terrible row. On our way home from school, my mother is wary and distant as I tag along beside her, my nine-year-old legs scarcely able to keep up to her furious pace. Supper is a grim, silent meal, my mother enclosed within herself and I, a timid child fearful of awakening furies, eating quietly and keeping my distance. In the April evening our neighbours are clearing away the detritus of winter, raking old leaves and twigs from flower beds and hedges. The air is fragrant with leaf smoke. I remember sitting in my bedroom in the enfolding darkness smelling that leaf smoke. The house was utterly still, for downstairs Mother too was sitting in the darkness, waiting for my father.

That afternoon she had been summoned from her class-room to the principal's office where a telephone call awaited her. The malice of some people is beyond belief. Who was the caller? The parent of a child who had received a failing grade on his Easter report? Someone anxious to remind Grace Wheeler that just because she teaches school, she is not as smart as she thinks she is with her fancy words and her phonograph records from Eaton's in Toronto. There is no shortage of people in small towns who are eager to remind you that you are no better than they are, and don't you forget it, Mrs. Know-It-All. Whoever it was, we shall never know. The identity of the caller remained one of those maddening puzzles that probably kept her awake at night imagining enemies everywhere.

The telephone call arrives at two o'clock in the afternoon. I see my mother leaving her classroom and going down to Mr. Ball's office accompanied by the principal's secretary, Mrs. Armitage. Fortunately, Mr. Ball is now teaching grade eight history, and so at least she will have the privacy of his office. The fact remains, however, that a telephone call has arrived in the middle of the teaching day, and this is cause for speculation on the part of Mrs. Armitage and all those whom she will doubtless tell. For Grace, the call can only mean bad news. Why else would someone interrupt your day's work unless to tell you about the car accident in which your husband now lies dead in a ditch, or the fire which at this very moment is consuming your home. The pessimist always steels herself for the worst tidings imaginable.

As she closes the door of the principal's office, she sees the phone like an open mouth on his desk. When she picks up the receiver and says, "Grace Wheeler speaking," she hears a muffled voice. Someone could be speaking through a handkerchief or a tea towel. The words themselves are like blows from a stranger, from a madwoman who suddenly appears on the street to strike you, disrupting your sense of how things ought to be. For a moment your wits are scattered to the four winds. What is happening here? Let me think!

"You should keep better tabs on your husband, Mrs. Wheeler. Do you know where he is at this moment?"

At such times, if only to gather our thoughts, we ask foolish questions.

"Who is this? Who is speaking?"

"Maybe you should ask your husband tonight where he spent his afternoon. And who with?"

It is difficult to maintain composure under such circumstances. But maintain it she must. I see her standing by Mr. Ball's desk looking out the window at the school yard on that sunlit April day, a tall serious woman about to enter her thirty-third year. Already there is a dryness beneath her eyes, a sexual aridity that foretells perhaps the spare elderly woman she will one day become. And now she must prevail; she must pass Mrs. Armitage's desk with this burden and return along the hallway to her classroom.

There is another hour and a half to be got through: sentences to be parsed, a geography lesson to be taught. The map of the world must be unfurled and the wooden pointer applied to faraway places with strange-sounding names. And the voice through the tea towel must be kept at bay.

"Maybe you should ask your husband tonight where he spent his afternoon. And who with?"

When my father comes home, I am in my bedroom across the hall from where I now sit, trying to assemble a balsa-wood Spitfire. I listen to the front door closing and the sound of his footsteps on the stairs. A few moments later I hear the outpouring of his water into the toilet bowl and the flushing. On his way downstairs, he opens my door and looks in, a grinning, boyish medium-sized man in sports jacket and trousers. No khaki uniform, no polished boots or puttees like the men in the Home Guard who train in the curling rink and march down King Street on Monday evenings. Other fathers are in the regular army, and one extraordinarily lucky boy has a father in the air force. My father sells used cars and plays cribbage while other men fight in the war or build Corvettes at the shipyard.

Was I thinking these contemptuous thoughts or was I merely annoyed by his grin? Why should he be in such a good humour when my mother and I are enveloped in such bitter silence? He picks up my pathetic little airplane and, after examining it, puts it back on my desk. He cannot help me and knows enough not to try. He asks me about my day, but I say nothing and only shrug. Ever my mother's son, I am punishing him for not shouldering his portion of the unhappiness in this house.

Standing in the hallway I hear their voices rising with the warm air from the furnace through the black iron squares of the heating vent. There is also the sound of dishes and cutlery as she places before him the supper of meat loaf and boiled potatoes and canned peas which has been warming in the oven.

"I had a phone call at school today." My mother sounds almost buoyant. The voice of the prosecutor with the evidence. *I've got the goods on you, Buster.* "Who is she?"

She? What does that mean? I stare at the black grates and the name of the ironmonger I now know by heart. Hawse and Sons Limited, Akron, Ohio. My mother's voice rises again through the warm air in my face.

"Is she one of those floozies who hang around the hockey team? Or some baggage from down around the coal docks?"

Floozies? Baggage? What did such words signify? At first I can't hear my father. I picture him bent over his meal proffering mild denials to the charges. I can catch only a few of his words.

"Now, Grace . . . all about? . . . town gossip . . . do you?"

A gentle falsehood turneth away wrath. But only sometimes. And not in this case. My mother's voice seems to move into a higher register as the angry, silent person finally will be heard.

"I will not stand for this. Not phone calls at the school. I simply will not tolerate . . ." Et cetera, et cetera.

A breaking point! The quiet guilty man has had enough and begins to see himself as an afflicted party. Persecuted beyond reason over his meat loaf and peas. In its bluntness and power, his outcry is all the more terrible since he seldom raises his voice in anger.

"Oh for Christ's sake, shut up and give me some peace!"

"Don't you dare use such language in this house, Ross Wheeler. I won't abide it."

Abide it! Mother's word power again! It sounds like a chair overturning, and then the kitchen door is slammed. Breathless I stand in the warm dark air from the grate listening to the car start up in the driveway. A few moments later I hear my mother running the tap and scraping the supper dishes, for always there must be someone to clean up after such scenes.

Who "she" was is never discovered, but the town is full of servicemen's wives and other grass widows whose husbands are working in Toronto factories, and who come home only on weekends. There are plenty of lonely women around. I came to believe, however, and still do, that it was the bleached blonde Irma Dawes. I saw her with my father once that summer and, putting the pieces together when I was older, concluded that "she" was Dawes's wife. One Saturday evening my father took me with him to the Sundee Apartments, a brick building from the 1920s on the west side of town. He was delivering Dawes's paycheque. Dawes was ill with mumps, and this childhood disease in an adult was cause for humour between Irma Dawes and my father.

"I hope they don't go down on him, Bud. What a tragedy!"

At nine years of age, I, of course, had no idea what they were referring to, but I glimpsed the patient through the open bedroom door. Dawes lay in bed with a grey swollen face. His thinning hair had not been combed and he looked quite bald and old. He waved to me. "Hi, Kiddo!" It came out a kind of croak.

Irma Dawes made a fuss over me. "Do you want a Coke, honey? I got lots of Coke in the icebox." She served my father a rye and ginger ale. When, years later at university, I read F. Scott Fitzgerald's *The Great Gatsby* and encountered Tom Buchanan's girlfriend, Mrs. Wilson, with her little dog and blowsy handsomeness, I realized that I had met her before in real life. She was Irma Dawes in her red shoes and tight skirt and sheer blouse. That Saturday evening she and my father traded jokes and seemed completely at ease in one another's company.

During those years my parents conducted the kind of familiar, pointless warfare so often undertaken by two people who no longer see much point in sharing space and time. Between skirmishes, there would be weeks of calm when Mr. and Mrs. Wheeler seemed like any other married couple, surprised on occasion by thoughtfulness, but rankled too by little cruelties and perceived shortcomings. In marriage there was much to endure, but weren't most people in the same boat? And wasn't divorce complicated and expensive? It's hard to believe nowadays, but your name was actually read aloud in the House of Commons.

Divorce was for movie stars and millionaires who didn't give a damn.

If my mother took refuge in the novels of Lloyd C. Douglas and A. J. Cronin, and the "Bell Telephone Hour," my father sought help from Old Dominion and the movies. In those days, you called it "going to the show." My father was always "going to the show." It was a place to escape from his wife's bitter silences, from George Fowler's smirk, from the man in the plaid shirt saying, "I don't think so, Bud. I believe I'll look around a bit more," from his own aging legs that with each passing winter were slowing him down on the ice. On Saturday nights he watched the Westerns. Hopalong Cassidy and Johnny Mack Brown and Lash LaRue. Through the week he enjoyed steamy melodramas starring beautiful dangerous women like Veronica Lake and Lana Turner.

I remember going to one of these with him. It was a Monday evening in the fall of that year of his philandering with Irma Dawes. He came home early. He had been drinking and there were words between them. He arose from the kitchen table and put on the sports jacket which he had draped across the back of his chair. My mother had tried in vain to break him of this habit. Standing in the kitchen, he asked me if I wanted to go to the early show with him. I was bewildered. After all, it was a school night, and there were dishes to dry and homework to do. This was most unorthodox and I looked at my mother who was still at the table finishing her tea. Whether she was just distracted, or merely wanted to be rid of the both of us for an hour or two, I shall never know. But she raised no objections to this adventure and said only, "I forbid you to drive that car in your condition, Ross. Not with Howard!"

Shrugging, my father tossed the car keys onto the kitchen table, and we walked out into the October evening.

A wind had arisen off the bay to scatter the leaves along the street, and it was cool as we walked past houses where behind lighted windows people were sitting down to their suppers. In his sports jacket and trousers, my father was as ill clad for the weather as he would be on another October night ten years later when he walked off with Lois Sparling on Dundas Street in Toronto.

"We'll go down to the Royal and have some pie and ice cream," he said. "Then we'll go the show. There's a good one on tonight with Barbara Stanwyck. A beautiful woman and a good actress too. How does that sound, Howie?"

I said it sounded fine. I was tremendously excited to be out on a Monday night with my father.

I had never been in the Royal Café. For many, including my mother, the Royal was considered not quite respectable. The high school kids preferred to drink their Cokes and milk shakes at the Green Parrot or Allen's Dairy Bar. No one would entertain the idea of having Sunday dinner at the Royal. It was for oilers and deckhands from the lake freighters who ate their hot chicken sandwiches there after a day of beer at the Huron House or snooker at Academy Billiards. At the Royal, Leo Kennedy could sit in a gumwood booth and coach a man who got drunk on Saturday night and socked his wife and now had to face his day in court. At the long counter at the front of the restaurant men who lived in rooms had their pie and coffee.

Such men knew my father and greeted him as we entered. They regarded me with a kind of detached curiosity as though trying to figure out who I was in the context of the Buddy Wheeler they knew. *Does Buddy have a kid? I never knew that.* We sat in a booth at the back, and my father ordered slices of lemon meringue pie with ice cream. When the waiter opened a swinging door to the kitchen, I saw an elderly man with a pigtail chopping vegetables with an immense knife.

That evening my father and I went to see James M. Cain's *Double Indemnity*, a classic 1940s tale of lust and murder. Barbara Stanwyck plays a ruthless floozy (to use my mother's word) who inveigles an insurance agent, Fred MacMurray, into knocking off her rich husband. The insurance man chokes the husband to death from the back seat of a 1938 LaSalle that was just like the one parked in the front row of the car lot on Bay Street with the price on the windshield. The crime is eventually solved by MacMurray's boss, Edward G. Robinson. What did I, at nine years of age, make of all that domestic treachery? I can't remember. I have since watched the movie a dozen times, and always I return to that October night, remembering especially the scattered leaves along the streets and the lemon meringue pie and the old Chinese cook with his pigtail.

Mrs. Chernyk, God bless her, has found a buyer for all this furniture. Last night the man came around and we settled on a figure and I gave him a key which he will return to Mrs. Chernyk's office. This weekend he will come by with his truck and take away all my mother's earthly possessions: the refrigerator and stove, the piano, the little secretary in the hallway, the kitchen chairs we sat on for innumerable meals, the dining-room and parlour furniture from Grandfather Stewart's house, the bed she slept in for sixty years; it will all disappear into the man's truck and this house will be as bare as it was on that July evening in 1934 when Grace Stewart walked around the large empty rooms with Rusty Robinson, frowning at the wallpaper and the grease stains in the kitchen.

I was thinking of this when my visitor arrived this afternoon. At the front door stood a man in his early thirties, sandy-haired with a moustache. He was wearing a tracksuit. With his trim figure and healthy glistening face, he looked like a gym teacher. I thought of a jogger new to the town seeking directions, but when I opened the door, he extended a hand and introduced himself in a clear tenor voice.

"Howard Wheeler? I'm Barry Lawson from Knox."

My face must have looked blank, for he quickly added, "I wrote you some weeks ago about your mother. Sorry I haven't managed to visit sooner, but Karen and I have been away all summer at a camp for young Christians. We just got back last week."

Ah yes! It was the young minster from Knox Presbyterian Church who had buried mother; the letter writer who didn't know the difference between the nominative and the objective cases.

I invited him in, asking if he minded the kitchen. I was thirsty for a bottle of beer. He didn't mind at all, and so we passed the doorway to the parlour where my mother used to serve tea and biscuits to Lawson's predecessors, among whom I especially remember Dr. Fordyce, a mild old man in black serge and clerical collar. At the end of his visits, he and my mother would bow their heads in prayer for this house and the safety of all who dwelt therein. Now the minister wore a tracksuit and we talked in the kitchen about running. I offered him a beer but he chose orange juice. He told me the juice replaced things lost in the body while running.

"I've changed my route," he said. "I usually run down in the park, but I thought I'd come over this way for a change and look in on you."

He smiled. He was a handsome fellow with his finely shaped head and gingery moustache. I could see him setting ablaze the hearts of various members of the Women's

Auxiliary when he dropped by the food bank on a Wednesday afternoon. He doubtless brightened the day of many an elderly widow at Birchmount Lodge.

"Well, how have you been anyway?" he asked as though already we were old friends.

"How do you mean?" I asked. "Physically?"

He spread his arms and grinned. "In every way, of course. The whole man!"

I could now see that it was his little joke. Ministering unto the whole man or something. I shrugged and took a swallow of beer.

"The whole man is not as whole as he used to be. However, I seem to be on the mend. You never know about these things of course. I'm seeing a doctor in Toronto tomorrow. A heart man."

He nodded. "That's great."

After finishing his orange juice he said, "My letter was quite inadequate. It didn't really convey my admiration for your mother, Howard."

I gathered that he was waiting for "Nice of you to say that, Barry," or some other dollop of conversational mortar that would set in place this instant familiarity so cherished nowadays by preachers and salesmen. I took another swallow of beer and said nothing.

"Of course," he said, "I only knew her during the last year of her life. But she was an impressive woman. So capable! I sensed a genuine strength in her."

"Yes, she was certainly strong," I said. "She had plenty of good old-fashioned Presbyterian strength."

Lawson had no ironical sense; we were talking, it seemed, about different things.

"She never missed a Sunday," he said. "Not even on the stormiest days of winter. It was really amazing." He looked around the kitchen. "And she took care of this big house by herself." He paused. "She was fortunate in a way, I guess. She missed all that nursing home stuff."

"Yes," I said. "Thank God for that."

"And all at eighty-one?"

"Eighty-two actually."

"Remarkable! I always enjoyed our little chats after Sunday morning worship. She was very stimulating company, your mother." He shook his head as though fondly remembering these occasions.

"If she didn't like something in one of my sermons, she would certainly let me know. And in no uncertain terms. So many seniors reach a certain age and then just give up. But that was not your mother's way." He continued to shake his head as though amazed. I guessed that mother had given him a hard time. "She certainly had her opinions, didn't she?" he said. "But she kept up with things and was very well read."

Opinionated, yes! She thought the French, among many other groups, were getting altogether too pushy. She believed that no one knew the value of a dollar any more. Like most old people, she saw a careless, spendthrift world that no longer made sense. Well read, no! Like many school-teachers, her taste in books was quite ordinary. After the biblical novels of her middle years, she favoured immense historical sagas filled with information and lifeless characters. In her old age, James Michener was her favourite writer. I can see how my daughter's taste in reading comes from her grandmother whose ideas about many things were formed early and scarcely wavered over a lifetime.

"She never mentioned your father, Howard," said Barry Lawson. "I gather he passed away some years ago."

"Yes, he did," I said. "In a flophouse in Toronto." I rather enjoyed his wide-eyed look of disbelief. "He was only in his mid-fifties," I continued. "Younger than I am now, which should give me pause. And, as a matter of fact, does." I held up my beer. "He was a little too fond of this. And stronger stuff of course. He died from a heart attack, probably aggravated by a cirrhotic liver. As you've probably noticed from the headstone, he's up there in Bayview too. My mother had his body brought back. So now they're together again, side by side, like the words in the old song."

"Pardon?"

"Nothing. A bad joke."

Lawson looked uneasy as though unable to decide whether he liked me or not. Yet was he not obliged to love all God's creatures however trying that might be? Out of sympathy perhaps he began to talk about a favourite uncle who had a drinking problem and died from it.

While I listened, I thought of my mother bringing home the body of the husband she had not seen for twenty-two years. The police had phoned to say they found her name in his billfold. She could have disowned him, saying with some justification that his funeral was not her responsibility; that after twenty-two years of silence and neglect, he had surrendered any claims on her attention. But she didn't. She took care of all the arrangements including the telegram I received in Exeter, England, where Gillian and I were on our honeymoon, staying with her parents. *Your Father Died Yesterday. Heart Attack. Funeral Here Tomorrow. Mother.* I have often wondered what went through her mind when she looked upon his face after all those years.

She wasn't one for revealing such things, of course, and when I asked her about the funeral some weeks later, she wasn't particularly forthcoming. I had driven up to Huron Falls alone; it was already evident that Gillian and Mother would never be at ease in one another's company. We sat at the kitchen table drinking tea while I asked her about the funeral. She told me about it in her usual spare way.

"There weren't many people," she said. "A few of your father's old cronies from the Huron House." *Cronies!* Not friends. How she could devalue people with a word! "Your aunts, of course, all crying buckets, especially Mildred. I understand he was borrowing money from her at the end. Why the woman didn't get him off the drink I'll never understand. There's plenty of help for that around nowadays." She took a sip of tea. "It was a poor day. Raining and thunder and lightning. Not a good day to be standing under all those trees up at the cemetery. The minister hurried things along which I thought made a great deal of sense."

I could see them gathered at the graveside on that rainy summer afternoon with the thunder rolling above the trees. My stout and amiable aunts would be tearful, holding handkerchiefs against their eyes, remembering perhaps their brother as he was on those brilliant winter mornings when they played hockey with him on the frozen bay by the coal yards. My father's old drinking companions would be middle-aged and worn; they were probably fidgeting, waiting for the minister to finish so they could get down to the legion. And I could see my mother standing next to the minister, solitary and austere in her black dress.

I appeared to be nodding in the right places as Lawson finished his story about the derelict uncle. When he got to his feet, he flexed his knees a little; apparently he intended to run all the way back to the manse on the other side of town. He looked down at his Reeboks, a tanned muscular Christian; you could see the sexual bulge in his track pants.

"I guess I better be on my way," he said. On the veranda he smiled at me. "I wonder, Howard, would you like to have dinner with us? I don't mean tonight of course, but one of these days. I make a terrific lasagna."

Why on earth, I wondered, would he want me to have dinner with him? It didn't take long to find out.

"Karen," he said, "is very interested in writing. Last winter she took this creative writing course at Georgian College. She drove down to Barrie every Tuesday night. Of course she studied English at Dalhousie too. She's always been interested in story writing. Anyway, she's been working on these stories for the past few months."

Here it was then, the real reason behind this visit from the man of God: his wife had a manuscript. One of the drawbacks to life in book publishing is that perfect strangers will pluck your sleeve at a party and ask you to read something ghastly. And not only strangers. During my thirty years in the business, I have lost a couple of good friends and an excellent cleaning woman because I could not help them gain entry to the world of letters.

"Karen realizes that it's not easy to get published these days," said Lawson.

"Indeed it isn't," I said with feeling. "And it's getting more difficult by the minute. We publish very little fiction any more."

Lawson's bright, eager smile betokened a man who was not yet convinced that most of these adventures have unhappy endings.

"These stories are really good, Howard. I think Karen has exactly caught Ontario small-town life and all its foibles."

Ah yes, I thought unkindly. The old small-town foibles. *A Book of Foibles!*

"What she'd really like to talk about is how to get published. Should she copyright her stories, for example? And she wonders if maybe she should have an agent."

I was looking at the schoolchildren as they walked along the street through the late summer afternoon. Some of them at least would be the grandchildren, perhaps even the great-grandchildren, of youngsters my mother had taught.

"An agent would be advisable," I said, thinking of how it nearly always came down to this hunger for recognition. Most people in my experience don't want to write so much as to be writers. Working with language to discover what words can and cannot do does not interest them half so much as those trappings of authorship that seem to them so enticingly glamorous: the luncheon with the agent, the photograph on the dust jacket, the autographing party at the department store, the interview on the CBC. I thought of Pettinger and his long retreat from all that.

"I'm afraid I won't be back in town for a while," I said.

Lawson still looked unabashedly hopeful.

"But you will have to come back sometime. You have to settle things here. Right?"

"Yes."

"Well, why not give us a call then? Karen is dying to meet you."

"We'll see."

"Terrific." He tapped me playfully on the chest. "And take care of that old ticker."

He adjusted something on the watch that lay across his wrist like a large silver coin.

"See ya, Howard," he called and, waving, took off, running lightly along the street, a man in a blue tracksuit, weaving among the schoolchildren, disappearing behind trees and finally around a corner.

DURING THE LAST SUMMER that he lived with us, my father's drinking sharply increased. It began with the celebration of VE-Day in May. What my father had to celebrate was hard to imagine. The war had been a remote event for him; like many civilians in towns like Huron Falls, he had actually prospered from it. Despite the gasoline rationing, people still wanted cars and any model in reasonable condition sold fairly quickly. George Fowler travelled down to London and Windsor, attending funerals and auctions, prying family sedans from flustered widows. In the lot on Bay Street, Earl Dawes and my father would sell them the following week. There was money in town. The shipyard had six hundred men building Corvettes; the woollen mill was turning out socks for the troops, and the grain elevators operated day and night unloading freighters from Port Arthur and Fort William.

At thirty-three my father was playing hockey for the Huron Falls Intermediates and, despite his drinking, was still the best player around. I watched a game that spring against an army team from Camp Borden. My Aunt Mildred was home for the weekend and we sat behind the players' benches. Before the game a pipe band in kilts played marches at centre ice. That night my father scored three goals in leading the Flyers to victory.

When word officially arrived on that May day that Germany had surrendered, the siren at the fire hall wailed and cars filled with high school kids drove along the streets with horns blaring. A parade was hastily assembled at the curling rink and marched downtown led by the Home Guard. I was in the Knox Church rhythm band playing "Christ Is Our Redeemer" on the back of an old Fargo truck on loan from the planing mill. From there I could see my father's blond head among the crowd that lined King Street. The head soon disappeared through the door of the Huron House. That night there were fireworks and crowds of young people surging back and forth throughout town, but it was all innocent, and beyond a few soaped store windows and overturned outhouses, no damage was done.

My mother stayed home and listened to the radio news. If people wanted to carry on like fools, there was precious little she could do about it. After a day or two of these high spirits, most people again took up their normal lives. My father, however, decided to continue the celebrations more or less all summer. And there were incidents. Now and then he didn't come home, and at noon the following day, my mother would have to stand in the hallway by the telephone.

"No, Mr. Fowler. He is not here. I have no idea where he is or why he is not at the lot. Yes, I'll have him call you when he comes in."

Those conversations must have been searingly painful for her. Then something happened at the Huron House, and my father was asked to do his drinking elsewhere. Now he no longer drank with Leo Kennedy or Chip McNeil, but with other men in the back seats of cars parked along country roads or by the coal yards. I used to wonder what went through my mother's mind while she lay alone through those summer nights waiting for him to come home: hearing finally at daybreak the slamming car door, the voices and laughter of men, her husband in the kitchen frying eggs. She must have turned and feigned sleep when he eased himself down beside her.

The gods then appeared to smile upon our household and my father was offered a job playing senior hockey in Nova Scotia. George Fowler, of course, was behind this, and it would be agreeable to imagine that he wanted to give my father one last chance to redeem himself. I think it more likely, however, that he saw this as an opportunity to get Buddy Wheeler off his hands. With the end of the war, new cars would soon be coming in, and Fowler wanted out of the used-car business. Whatever his motives, he invited my father to his cottage on Go Home Bay one Sunday in the middle of August to meet the owner of the team. Not only that, but Fowler wanted my mother and me to come along, perhaps to convey the impression that Buddy Wheeler was a family man.

I was ten years old and this was an event, a boat ride through the Thirty Thousand Islands. My mother, probably guessing Fowler's intentions and oddly allied with him in wanting to make this thing work, even gave up church that morning since the *Huron Queen* left at ten o'clock, steaming from the harbour, leaving in her wake a stream of thick black smoke from the soft coal she burned.

The *Huron Queen* was filled with people from Toronto. To get away from the sticky heat and the polio scares of the city in August, they spent a week or two in Huron Falls, renting cabins at Little Lake Park or rooms in tourist homes. They were Jewish, the families of men who owned dress factories on Spadina Avenue and Sullivan Street. The factory owners in their slacks and short-sleeved shirts leaned against the railing and smoked White Owls, staring out at the shoreline of Georgian Bay. After five minutes they descended to the lounge to play pinochle. On the upper deck, their wives, handsome and tanned in sun-dresses, talked about their children who raced about the ship eating egg salad sandwiches and drinking Coca-Cola. They were loud and exuberant people, and beside them, my parents and I seemed lifeless and pale, a family of tepid WASPS voyaging in the strange waters of the Levant even if we were in the heartland of Ontario.

At Honey Harbour, we gawked at the Delawanna Inn and the Royal Hotel where guests sat in wooden lawn chairs reading books and newspapers. We passed within a hundred feet of rocky treeless islands, and on one of these enormous boulders, a painfully thin woman the colour of burnt cork was performing a series of calisthenics or ballet exercises. There was no cottage or boat; only this woman exercising in the raw sunlight, and I wondered how she got there or left. As we passed, she raised her eyes and arms to the sky gods, and even as a child, I could sense something studied about her performance. It seemed a kind of spiritual striptease for a boatload of tourists. I was also watching one of the deckhands; he was smoking a cigarette and coiling a length of rope. His expression suggested that he had seen it all before.

Many years later at a party, I mentioned this excursion and the exercising woman to the poet A. L. Sims who had been talking about his childhood summers among the islands of Georgian Bay. A year or two passed and then I recognized in a new collection of his work a poem entitled "Woman on a Rock." He had put in the woman and the sunlight and the rock, the boatload of Jewish tourists with their egg salad sandwiches and Coca-Cola, the deckhand with his cigarette and coil of rope. He had left me out and placed an older narrator in the poem along with an absent lover and a vague reference to the war in Europe and the Holocaust. "Woman on a Rock" is, I believe, still popular in poetry anthologies for high school students.

At noon we pulled into the wharf at Go Home Bay where Fowler was waiting for us wearing a short-sleeved white shirt, dungarees and a captain's cap. He was accommodating, even cordial. "Nice to see you and the young fellow, Mrs. Wheeler," he said. My mother nodded. She could never bring herself to wear the wide loose-fitting trousers that had become popular with women during the war, and so she had chosen a summer dress and white shoes. She looked awkward and prim as Fowler helped her into his boat, a mahogany launch with an inboard engine. I sat in the stern and watched the propeller churn the oily rainbow-coloured water as we surged forth. My mother sat beside me, holding down the dress around her legs, the kerchief on her head flapping in the wind. In front of us Fowler, in his dungarees and white-peaked cap, looked like the skipper as he steered his boat and talked to my father.

There is a picture of the three of us, taken that day by one of Fowler's guests, a big sandy-haired man from Cleveland, Ohio, who owned hockey teams and racehorses. He could see that my mother and I were out of place in that company of sportsmen, and so he took a kindly interest in us. To amuse me, he performed simple tricks with a large silver coin that I badly wanted to own. It was an American fifty-cent piece, and he could make it disappear between his thick fingers, and then pluck it from his ear in a manner that delighted me. At the end of his performance, he gave me the coin, and for the rest of the afternoon, I clenched a fist around it in the pocket of my short pants.

The sandy-haired man was interested in my mother's profession. I heard him tell her that his mother had been a teacher and that he would like to have been one too, a statement I considered outlandish and probably untrue, one of those harmless adult falsehoods that are used in conversation to flatter and ingratiate. I had reached an age where teaching is seen as a rather contemptible occupation. I had overheard boys my age talking about "crabby old Mrs. Wheeler" and "smelly Hepworth" and "Baldy Ball," and I was inclined to agree with the school yard ethos that all teachers, including my mother, represented a particular kind of enemy. Besides, teaching was a woman's job, so why would any man other than the likes of Baldy Ball want to be a part of it? Yet the man from Ohio seemed in earnest as he asked my mother about her early years in teaching, smiling readily with a large face that looked ravaged and sore from the broken capillaries along the cheekbones. Looking back, I now realize that he was probably a recovering alcoholic who had chosen for safety's sake to be near a non-drinker.

Fowler's spacious cottage was made of cedar shakes painted dark green. It had a big screened-in veranda that overlooked the water and was surrounded by pine trees. A carpet of their dead needles covered the rocky surface. With her usual suspicion that misfortune was imminent, Mother warned me about rattlesnakes and I explored the island warily, clutching the half-dollar coin in my pocket. I was the only child at the party and was mostly ignored as I wandered among the guests. The men were middle-aged or older; stout and prosperous they stood in groups talking about hockey teams in places like New Haven, Connecticut, and St. Paul, Minnesota. Their wives and girlfriends sat in striped canvas lawn chairs drinking gin and lime rickey and chatting about boat trips on the Great Lakes and movie stars and the Woolworth heiress, Barbara Hutton, who was getting married again. I watched my father sipping a beer and laughing with the owner of the team from Nova Scotia.

A pretty young woman in a yellow bathing suit came out of one of the cabins by the side of the cottage and, carrying her towel and bathing cap, walked past us down to the dock. Everyone seemed to stop talking as she went by. We all watched her dive into the water and swim for a few minutes before giving it up; it is never much fun swimming by yourself, and so she tore off her bathing cap and climbed the stone steps towards us looking surly. Later in the afternoon she would drink too much and create a fuss before being hustled into the cabin by an older man.

Fowler moved easily among his guests, the genial host waving his cigar and slapping people on the back. Remembering him from that long ago August afternoon has helped me to imagine the Christmas party in the Huron House during the first year of my parents' marriage.

Inside the cottage two women who looked like nurses in their white uniforms had laid out a buffet supper. Guests sat on the veranda behind the screened windows balancing plates of ham and potato salad on their knees or laps. The walls of the cottage were covered with framed autographed pictures of old hockey players crouched unsmiling over their sticks. They looked tough enough to take off your head if you got in their way: Dutch Gainor, Butch Keeling, Buzz Boll, Dit Clapper, Cy Wentworth, Red Dutton, Sweeney Schriner, Johnny Gottselig, Earl Seibert. My father had played against some of these men, and as he and the owner from Nova Scotia passed beneath each photograph, they would stop and discuss the merits of each player. My father was behaving very well that day.

Before she got drunk, the girl who had been swimming came into the cottage looking scrubbed and pert in her sweater and white shorts. It was hard to ignore her as she stood by a phonograph, swaying and snapping her fingers to the music.

> You've got to ac-cent-tchu-ate the positive
> E-lim-in-ate the negative
> Latch on to the af-firm-a-tive
> Don't mess with Mr. In-between

It was shortly after this that the big sandy-haired man took our picture. We stood outside on the brown needles as the sun poured light through the pine trees. In the background is the cottage veranda, and you can just see a few dark figures behind the screens. My father has his arms around the both of us and is smiling. And why not? Isn't it Sunday afternoon and a time for drinks and fellowship and stories of old heroes? Monday is still hours away. My mother seems apprehensive as though expecting the crystal to shatter at any moment. *Doesn't it always?* Beside them I look small and watchful in my striped T-shirt and short pants and brush cut.

In the late afternoon Fowler took us back in his launch to the wharf where we again boarded the *Huron Queen* for the journey homeward. Again, we passed the boulder where the woman had stretched forth her arms to the sun. But now she was nowhere to be seen. Had an indulgent father fetched her back to the cottage for an evening of Chinese checkers with Mom and Dad? Subdued perhaps by food and drink and the drenching sunlight of the long summer day, passengers now talked quietly among themselves. Some of the men were asleep in deck chairs, a fist mashed against a cheek, a dead cigar in the other hand. My parents sat in the lounge talking softly. Now, on the eve of a twenty-two-year separation, they seemed at last unburdened and at ease with one another, almost happy together.

After a while I grew bored in the lounge and climbed the iron stairs to the upper deck to lean against the railing. There I was joined by a boy who told me his name was Sammy. He was my height but nearly twelve, with curly, dark hair and a sturdy build. Soon we were seeing who could spit farther over the railing. I longed to show him my American half-dollar, but I was cautious and fearful that one of us might drop the coin. I could see it clattering against the deck before rolling into the dark green water where already the white tendrils of our saliva were disappearing to become a part of something else.

Sammy asked me what I thought of the atomic bomb, and I told him that I had never heard of such a thing. He looked at me scornfully. Didn't I read the newspapers, or listen to the radio news? The Americans, he told me, had this new super weapon called an atomic bomb. One of them could destroy an entire city, and in fact that very week the Americans had blown up two Japanese cities called Hiroshima and Nagasaki. Two bombs! Two cities! He invited me to imagine the power of such a weapon, but I couldn't. For me, the war had been with Germany and they were now defeated; Japan had always seemed more like America's enemy than ours. What Sammy told me sounded fantastic and remote. It had happened on the other side of the world, far away from the deep green water and the rocky islands and the lighted evening sky of summer over Georgian Bay.

DR. KHAN STILL USES a fountain pen to write prescriptions, and even at such ordinary tasks, his slender brown hand looks deft and quick. It is, of course, a surgeon's hand, and can guide a needle through an artery to the human heart. I have spent the morning wired to various machines while I trod the treadmill and pedalled the stationary bicycle. My test results appear to be satisfactory though Dr. Khan has said nothing; I believe he wants me to interpret his silence as approval. Dr. Khan has the specialist's air of priestly condescension towards laymen, but I also detect a kind of mild contempt for Western attitudes. His manner seems to suggest that we Canadians overvalue our perceived singularity. We perhaps make too much of personal suffering. If you had seen what I have seen on the streets of Calcutta! That sort of thing!

"Continue with the medication, Mr. Wheeler," says Dr. Khan, "and please make an appointment to see me in three months. You are making satisfactory progress. The usual injunctions apply of course. Watch your diet and exercise moderately. A brisk daily walk is probably best for someone your age."

"Can I go back to work?"

Dr. Khan places his long dexterous fingers on the desk as though it were a piano awaiting his sonata.

"I don't see why not. You are in the book publishing business, aren't you? I should try to avoid stressful situations if I were you."

"Of course. Thank you, Dr. Khan."

As I get to my feet, he nods unsmiling.

"No problem, Mr. Wheeler."

It is easy to get lost in the Toronto Hospital. You must be attentive to the signs in the corridors as you pass the shuffling patients in their housecoats, the doctors with their clipboards, the orderlies with their hampers of soiled linen, the rooms where men and women hooked up to bags of blood lie sleeping. How grave the suffering look while they sleep! Has the pain, I wonder, even invaded their dreams? In the last days of his life, Del was heavily drugged and often asleep when I dropped by Casey House after work to see him. Sometimes he was still wearing his Walkman, and you could hear faintly the Cole Porter songs, "I Get a Kick Out of You," "Love for Sale," "Just One of Those Things." On his bed lay copies of the *New Yorker*, and on the table beside him stood the vase of yellow roses his mother brought each week.

I am happy to open the glass door of the hospital and come out onto University Avenue into a windy bright autumn day. The traffic is dense, and there are plenty of empty taxis. It is nearly one o'clock, and I don't want to be late for my luncheon with Pettinger. The driver is from the

Middle East, an Iranian, I think. He is listening to a cassette or is tuned in to an ethnic station; the sound of a reedy flute winds through the perfumed air of his Pontiac. The car smells of hair oil from another time, Brylcreem or Vitalis. For me, it is a poignant scent from the past. It is the smell of my father's baseball cap hanging on a doorknob in the kitchen while he ate an early supper. It is the smell of our bathroom after he worked a few drops of this stuff into his coarse blond hair and went off to sell used Buicks. The Iranian has a slack heavy face and seems half-asleep, though in fact he's an excellent driver, wheeling us around the delivery vans as we circle Queen's Park and travel north past the museum to the Park Plaza where Del used to take writers for drinks in the Roof Bar.

The Prince Arthur Room is busy with American tourists, and I am glad that Linda Macklin booked a table. It is still a few minutes to one and there is no sign of Pettinger. Seated near the window I can look out at the bright gusty afternoon. To prepare myself for Pettinger, or to celebrate Khan's all clear, I order a martini, an old favourite from my drinking days, remembering how I once invited my mother to have lunch in this dining room. Ten years ago. She no longer felt confident driving in Toronto and had come down from Huron Falls by bus for a medical appointment. She would not talk to me about her problem, and so I surmised it had something to do with the mysterious world of female genitalia. You didn't discuss such things with your son. Whatever it was, it eventually corrected itself. Following her appointment, I met her in the lobby of the Medical Arts Building and we walked along Bloor Street to this hotel. She was then in her seventies, a tall, strong woman, her grey hair still cut short and barbered severely behind her neck. She quickly dismissed my suggestion that we eat in this room.

"Why spend all that money, Howard?" she said. "It's far too extravagant. I only need a sandwich and a cup of tea. Murray's will be fine."

And so we ate in the coffee shop at the front of the hotel. Her life had been governed by thousands of similar decisions. You were not put on this earth to be prodigal with your time and money. You can wait for your celebration in heaven. Meanwhile, let forbearance be your watchword throughout the journey! With the brutal irony that so often informs our lives, she chose a man for whom restraint was impossible. In this story of their life together, I have tried to be fair to both.

At the end of his vast, heroic failure, Pettinger suggests that our century has destroyed the efficacy of such stories. The revolutions, the wars, the death camps, the collapse of our sense of community, the billions now swarming across the planet have made meaningless any account of two individuals' lives. It is, I suppose, another version of the heart specialist's view of things. Yet does there not persist within each of us a need to know and understand who we are and where we came from? And how else but through memory and imagination and language can we recount what might have happened yesterday or what may happen tomorrow?

Beyond the window a man hurries along Prince Arthur

Avenue. He is wearing a topcoat that is too narrow in the shoulders and too short for his long legs. On his head is one of those wide Tilley hats that you imagine men wearing on safaris. It is Pettinger and he stops to look through the window, cupping his hands against the sides of his face. It is an odd thing to do, one of those gestures that appear normal only to the eccentric or the self-assured. For a moment Pettinger gazes through the glass at the tourists and at me and then hurries away. A few moments later he is standing at the entrance to the dining room, holding his broad white hat and leaning forward, an elderly writer peering into a crowded room. I am waving to get his attention.